D0896603

When the Sky Rained Dust

—⁓⦿⦿⦿⦿⦿⁓—

Patrick Dearen

EAKIN PRESS ✺ Austin, Texas

"Down the Old Road to Home" (song), written by Carey
L. Harvey and Jimmie Rodgers. Copyright 1934 Peer
International Corporation. Copyright renewed. Used
by permission. All rights reserved.

FIRST EDITION
Copyright © 2004
By Patrick Dearen
Published in the United States of America
By Eakin Press
A Division of Sunbelt Media, Inc.
P.O. Drawer 90159 ⌨ Austin, Texas 78709-0159
email: sales@eakinpress.com
💻 website: www.eakinpress.com 💻
ALL RIGHTS RESERVED.
1 2 3 4 5 6 7 8 9
1-57168-830-7

Library of Congress Cataloging-in-Publication Data
Dearen, Patrick.
    When the sky rained dust / Patrick Dearen– 1st ed.
        p.   cm.
    Summary: Fourteen-year-old Josh faces love, a dust storm, and the
threat of losing his family's farm during the days of the Dust Bowl
and the Great Depression in 1934.
    ISBN 1-57168-830-7 (alk. paper)
        1. Depressions–1929–Ficiton. [1. Depressions–1929–Ficiton.
2. Dust storms–Ficiton. 3. Farm life–Texas–Fiction. 4. Texas–
History–1846-1950–Fiction. 5. Christian life–Fiction.] I. Title
PZ7.D3516Wh 2004
[Fic]–dc21   2004005150

For

Gwen Dell Dearen (1942-78), my sister,
who heard this story before I wrote it;

Ben and Diana Ramon,
friends and blessings beyond compare; and

John Cherry Watson (1909-94),
who guided me through the first draft
all those years ago.

Contents

Chapter 1

A Decent Chance

Pa roused me early on that morning that headed me once and for all down the road to manhood. The Central Texas sun had just peeped over the scorched live oaks when we started for Pettit in the wagon. As our mule team traced the dirt lane away from our farm, the dust rose in a fine powder and settled across a dry and thirsty land.

Maybe you don't know what drouth is. I was just four-teen that spring of 1934, but I knew plenty. This blight was like kerosene to an ant, or a fly swatter to a fly. The only difference was that dry-land farmers like Pa took a lot longer to kill. And drouth wasn't the only wolf at our door. Jobs and money were so scarce from coast to coast that folks were calling this "the Great Depression."

My days had never been so dark.

We hadn't gone far when Pa, a raw-boned man with graying temples, laid the reins across the frayed knee of his overalls and tore himself a chaw of Brown's Mule tobacco. His leathery face was drawn and his eyes were tired, as if he hadn't slept well in a long, long time.

"Wonder what your grandpa'd say, Josh, seein' the fix I got things in," he said.

"I . . . I'm worried, Pa."

"No use worryin' about somethin' the Good Lord's got control of," he said, stuffing the chaw in his mouth. "They either give us more time to pay it, or they don't. I know your ma and I did right. Long as Susie's okay, don't guess it matters if it costs us everything we got."

Both of us knew we were in big trouble. My little sister had been born sickly, and eighteen months ago Pa had borrowed against the farm to pay for an operation the doctors had said couldn't wait. Susie had come through it fine. But then a dry spell had spread through Comanche County and the peanut crop hadn't made. By that fall, drouth had taken a stranglehold on these post oak hills. After a hard winter without even a snow, our fields were bare and cracked.

If the rains didn't come soon, we wouldn't make a crop again this year, and we wouldn't have the money to make those payments at the bank. We stood to lose everything— our old house with warped cedar shingles, our bony cows, our seventy acres of dusty fields and briary oak thickets. My grandfather had spent out his life on that plot of dirt, and it had always been home to us two kids. I just couldn't imagine living anywhere else.

Soon we reached Pettit, which was what folks called a "one-horse" town. That meant it was mighty small, with barely enough activity to keep a single horse busy. The main street was caliche dirt, and most of the buildings were vacant and sagging. We passed Sam Morgan's general store and stopped under a live oak across from Pettit Bank. An old two-story rock structure, it hovered over us threateningly as we followed the line of flat rocks to the door.

Pa took off his worn felt hat and spat out his chaw. He took a long, hard look at the cloudless sky and wiped his brow. With the kind of sigh that a man like Pa shoves aside his pride with, he reached for the doorknob, and we went in.

We followed the *click-click* of a typewriter to the counter, where Pa rested his forearms on the edge and folded one worn boot behind the other. A middle-aged woman with tiny earrings turned around from a desk beyond.

"Mornin', ma'am," Pa said politely. "I'm Luke Watson. I need to see Mr. Hodgkins mighty bad."

"Why, certainly," she said, rising.

She entered an office behind the desk. I studied the scuffed path leading to that door and wondered how many other struggling farmers had made that walk in the past few months. I had a bad feeling about this, but I did my best to reassure myself. These were hard times. Jobs and money were scarce everywhere, and the dust in these parts was growing bitterer by the day. Surely the banker would see that and give us more time to pay up.

Still, I knew that these were the very reasons the bank might turn us away cold.

A balding, heavy-set man with bow tie came out, and Pa got right to the point.

"Mornin', Mr. Hodgkins. I ain't gonna have the money

to pay my way out of debt next week and you gotta help me out."

Hodgkins' thick eyebrows came together as he frowned. He sucked on his teeth and, like Pa, didn't mince words. "Banks are failing everywhere, Luke. We just can't absorb bad loans the way things are. I know this dry spell's created some problems for people. But like I told you before I started foreclosure proceedings, I just can't hand out special favors. If I was to give you an extension, I'd have to give one to everybody."

Pa slammed down his fist. "I ain't askin' no special favors! All I want's a decent chance!"

My father wasn't one to beg or make small-talk. He had made himself clear, and so had Hodgkins. In Pa's mind, there was nothing else to discuss. Whirling, he stormed away, leaving Hodgkins standing there with his mouth open. I gave the banker a last look and followed close behind. I'd never seen Pa so reddened by anger, and it went with him out into the sunlight.

He stood there, breathing heavily, and stared at the sweat-stained hat in his trembling hands. I was more worried about him than even the farm, and I searched for words to lift his spirits.

"Pa? Pa, isn't today . . . Ma's birthday?"

Only then did he find my eyes. "About forgot it, Josh." He put on his hat and glanced up the street. "Don't know if Sam will carry our account any further. If I was him, I wouldn't. But I'll mosey on up to his store and have a look-see for your ma if you'll run get those envelopes for her."

He handed me some pocket change and I headed for the

post office. As I passed the barber shop, a small sheet-metal building with striped pole outside, Al Burke came out sporting a new haircut. One of Pa's best friends, he owned the farm just west of ours. He was a clean-featured man with curly brown hair and the bluest eyes I'd ever seen.

"Say, Josh! Luke in town this mornin'?"

"Yes, sir. He's over at the general store."

"Good! Been tryin' to catch him for the past couple of days. Thanks, Josh."

He turned and headed for Sam's store, a dry wind tugging at his shirt.

Once inside the red-brick post office, I headed for the mailboxes without glancing at the counter. I had just inserted a key in our box when I heard the stamp of a little foot.

"Well, I like that! He walks right on by and won't even speak to me!"

I turned and found Al Burke's fourteen-year-old daughter Shan behind me. She had deep blue eyes, an ash-blond ponytail, and the sweetest smile of anyone I'd ever met. She may have been dressed like a boy—plaid shirt and threadbare jeans—but during the last couple of months, I had noticed a change coming over her.

She was a girl, and a mighty pretty one at that.

Her cheeks had a lot of color as she threw her hands to her hips. "Well? The cat got your tongue?"

"Oh, h-hi, Shan," I stammered. "I-I didn't see you."

I didn't understand what was happening to me. I'd known Shan for years, but only recently had I felt like a bumbling idiot around her.

"Oh, sure you didn't," she teased. "Sure."

"J-Just saw your dad outside," I said, conscious of her slight perfume. "S-Seemed like he wanted to see Pa awful bad."

"Well, you're who I've been wantin' to see. What've you been doin' since school let out, hidin' in the back thicket?"

When I wasn't able to manage any reply except for grinning like a possum, she poked me in the shoulder.

"Why don't you ever come over anymore and go horse-back ridin'?" she pressed.

I felt my face flush, and I looked down and smoothed out an imaginary dust spot with my boot. "Aw, just ain't got around to it lately. But I . . . I promise I'll . . . be over before long."

She hit me playfully in the shoulder again. "You better! If you don't, you're liable to see me come ridin' up to your front gate leadin' ol' Donner."

I looked up. "Oh, no! My backside still hurts from those prickly pears he dumped me in!"

She laughed heartily at that, and I grinned like a possum again. But once the mirth was over, I didn't know what to say. So I glanced at the mailbox and mumbled. "Guess I . . . I'll check the mail. See you later."

"Well, I like that!" she exclaimed, once more throwing her hands to her hips. "Already tryin' to get rid of me!"

Now I was more speechless than ever. I went ahead and checked the box, finding a letter from Aunt Mildred in Dallas. When I turned again, I saw that Shan hadn't budged an inch. I fidgeted with the letter and then summoned all my nerve.

"Uh ... your dad. He went over to Mr. Morgan's store. Pa's there. I, you, uh ..."

"Well, let's go, silly!"

All the way to Sam's, I asked myself just why I hadn't been to see Shan in so long—and why I was so nervous around her. For years we had ridden and roamed and I'd never thought a thing about it. But now, somehow, I could tell there were other things in life besides homegrown peas and barns full of peanut hay.

On the covered porch outside the weather-beaten store, we found Pa and Shan's dad talking and spitting tobacco juice. Mr. Burke looked up.

"Oh, Shannon," he said. "Better go pick out that fryin' pan you been houndin' me about."

Pa was still looking awfully worried, but he managed to muster a smile for Shan as we went in.

The wood floor creaked and Sam Morgan looked up from a cane-bottom chair. A hawk-faced old gentleman with horn-rimmed glasses and reddish-gray hair, he sat stuffing tobacco in his pipe.

"Howdy, son, girl," he said, having forgotten our names as usual.

He lit his pipe, and the odor of tobacco smoke followed us as we roamed the aisles. Shan located an iron skillet, while my eyes lighted up at a pair of ladies' stockings. I knew Ma would love them.

"Hey, look at these!" I exclaimed, holding them up.

"Oh, how pretty! They for your mother?"

I found the nerve to tease Shan a bit. "Naw, Pa and me

decided to start wearin' stockings out in the pasture instead of pants."

A touch of scarlet came to her cheeks. "Josh, you make me so mad sometimes!"

"Well, who else you think they'd be for besides Ma?"

She smiled impishly. "Well, I thought you might have some girl in mind."

It was my turn to blush. "Aw, quit your kiddin'."

More ill at ease than ever, I hurried straight for the cash register and the relative safety of Sam. About the same time, Pa and Mr. Burke came in.

"Well, howdy there, Luke, Al!" said Sam. "Thought that was y'all out there. How's things goin' this mornin'?"

"Not so good, Sam," said Pa, his face more drawn than ever. "Just got the door slammed in my face over at the bank."

"Oh? About your mortgage?"

Pa nodded. "I got my neck on the choppin' block, and that banker's swingin' a mighty big ax."

"Won't they give you a little more time?"

"Huh! He wouldn't give air to a drownin' dog."

Sam glanced at the pipe in his hand. "Sure sorry, Luke. If there's anything I can do . . ."

Pa breathed sharply. "Even if I was to square up with the bank somehow, it wouldn't fix things. If it don't rain . . ."

Pa wandered away, shaking his head. About that time Shan came up with the skillet and urged her dad to buy it. Mr. Burke nodded, and Sam limped over to fix up a charge ticket.

"Don't guess you've heard, Sam," said Mr. Burke, signing the IOU. "A bunch of us wrote our state representative about gettin' some government help in this drouth. He's supposed to be over at Hilldale Church tonight to talk to us farmers about it."

"Oh?" said Sam, raising an eyebrow. "Think it'll do any good?"

"Got to try somethin'. How about comin' over? Luke and all the rest are gonna be there."

"Hilldale Church, you say? We'll see about it," Sam said without committing. He sacked the skillet and handed it to Shan. "She a pretty good cook, Al?"

Mr. Burke exchanged glances with Shan. "Ever' bit as good as her mother was. Well, guess we better go."

Shan nudged me in the ribs with the sacked utensil. "Now, don't you forget about comin' over! You'd look funny wearin' this fryin' pan on your head!"

"I uh . . . I . . ."

"Bye-bye, Josh!"

They went out and Pa came up behind me, catching me staring after her. "Mighty pretty girl that Shannon Burke is," he remarked.

I sighed. "She's that for a fact."

"Guess she'll be at the meetin' tonight."

My face lighted up, and I craned for one last glimpse of that swinging ponytail through the window.

I couldn't wait till sundown!

Chapter 2

Turkey Buzzards

Things looked awfully bleak around the farm when we pulled through the wire-gap gate at the two big post oaks beside the lane. A hot, dry wind was blowing, and dust raced down the rows of bare fields. Over by the tin-roofed barn, the whirring windmill was screeching, laboring hard to find water. Past it, I could see our broken-down Model T Ford up on blocks, and the pasture with its gray nubs of grass and browning oaks and mesquites.

Down in the rickety pens, six bony cows tore at a bale of hay. I singled out a red-and-white crossbred we called "ol' Sal." She had been a milk pen calf and was as tame as a dog. She craved attention like a regular pet, and we all treated her as such. Sal started ambling up to meet us, as she often did.

As Pa pulled the wagon up beside the old two-story house and set the brake, I stared at the peeling paint, cracked windows, and sagging roof. I couldn't believe that we might be about to lose it all. These rotting planks and warped cedar shingles were *home.*

I climbed off, and motley-faced Sal was there to greet me. I took a moment to say a few words to the poor old thing and to rub her curly white poll. It sure hurt me to see her ribs protruding the way they were.

While Pa unhitched the team, I waded through the chickens and went in the back door. Ma was sweeping the kitchen with a broom Pa had fashioned from broomweeds.

"Y'all done back, Josh?" she asked wearily. Ma had always been small, but lately she seemed frail. Her hair, done up in a bun, was becoming streaked with gray, and the skin sagged under her eyes. Her complexion was beginning to tell of her many years in the sun.

"Hi, Ma."

"What did y'all find out?"

Inside, I sank. "Let Pa tell you."

Now there was a lot of worry in her eyes. Leaning the broom against the firewood box, she went to the door and peered out. Sal was standing there, staring in at us.

"He's unhitchin' the mules," I told Ma. Then I remembered the mail in my hand. "Oh, here's a letter from Aunt Mildred in Dallas."

Ma turned, the lines still deep in her face. "Did you get my envelopes?"

"Oh, no! I plumb forgot them! Pa gave me the money, but when I got to the post office I ran into Shannon Burke and forgot all about it."

"Oh?" she said, raising an eyebrow. "Since when's a girl make *you* forget somethin'?"

"Oh, Ma," I said, embarrassed.

Her eyes sparkled for just a moment. "I don't know—maybe Al's girl *would* turn a young man's head."

Pa came in.

"Luke, what happened at the bank?" Ma asked. "Josh wouldn't tell me."

Pa brushed past and tossed his hat on the table. "We ain't got a chance in the world, Sarah."

Ma laid a hand on his shoulder. "You mean they won't give us no more time? Oh, Luke! What are we gonna do?"

Pa hung his head. "I don't know. I just don't know."

I groped for something to say. "There's the meetin' tonight, Pa."

There wasn't much hope in Pa's voice as he told Ma about it. But she gave him an encouraging hug and told him the Good Lord was still looking out for us.

Ma cooked her own birthday supper that evening, and it was a dandy—pinto beans, cornbread with home-churned butter, and chocolate cake. After I set the table, she let little Susie ring the cowbell at the back door and Pa came in. He picked Sue-Sue up as he always did and asked, "How's my little girl doin'?" Too young to understand our troubles, she giggled, and even Pa smiled.

I swear that Susie, like Shan, was the cutest thing this side of Heaven. She had just turned three, and was she a little rascal! She had curly blond locks that fell to the shoulders of a flour-sack dress. Everywhere she went, she clutched a little button-eyed doll that I'd made for her out of socks and straw. No one had to tell us that the Lord had really blessed us when He had brought Sue-Sue into our lives.

Just after Pa returned thanks, he handed Ma a paper sack he had made fast with a string.

"What's this, Luke?" she asked.

"Go on and open it, Ma," I urged.

She tore it open, and when her eyes fell on the sleek stockings, she couldn't contain her excitement.

"Luke! We can't afford these! But they *are* wonderful!"

"Well, they're for a wonderful person," he said, smiling.

"They sure are!" I agreed.

And then little Susie, at the top of her tiny voice, shouted, "Happy buf-day, Mama!"

At dusk we pulled up to the little church set back in the live oak mott. We went inside to a lamplit sanctuary alive with milling folks and dancing shadows. All our neighbors were there, but there was just one person I wanted to see—Shan!

As I tried to squeeze through the crowd without seeming impolite, somebody poked me in the ribs.

"Well, howdy there, Josh, ol' boy!"

It was tall and lanky Wally Fingers, whose pride and joy was his handlebar mustache with its steer-horn curves. I think he'd spent his entire twenty-one years cultivating it. He leaned close and whispered.

"Got some moonshine out in the wagon. What say we slip off for a little nip?"

"Oh, Wally," I said, laughing. Then I spotted Shan and craned for a better look.

"Well, now!" exclaimed Wally, following my gaze. "Appears to me you got better things on your mind!"

Too embarrassed to respond, I edged away to his laughter.

Soon I was next to Shan, her perfume wafting over me. Boy, did she look like a million dollars in that blue dress with red belt! For the second time that day, I was reduced to a babbling idiot.

"Hi, Shan. I-I ... you, uh ... we ..." I lowered my gaze, scared out of my wits.

"Hi, Josh!"

My mouth went dry and my heart began pounding a hundred times a minute. Then she put her hand on my upper arm and I must've jumped three feet. But at least it brought my gaze up.

"I, uh ... did you ... ," I stammered.

"I've gotta go talk to Dad a minute. Save me a place to sit, okay?"

"I-I ..."

"I'll be lookin' for you!" Then she was away through the throng.

I backed away, a little stunned, and bumped into Wally.

"Hey, Josh, ol' boy! You're mumblin' and stumblin' like you done *had* some of that 'shine!"

I beat a fast path for Pa and found him with Sam Morgan. They were with a short, dark-suited stranger with so much grease in his hair I could see the lamplight in it.

"Mr. Peterson," Sam was telling the stranger, "there's a fellow here, good friend of mine, I'd like you to meet."

Peterson turned to smile broadly—a little too broadly, I thought. His breath smelled of garlic. "Always glad to meet one of my constituents."

Pa extended his hand. "Watson's my name, Luke Watson. You our representative?"

The lawmaker shook Pa's hand long and hard. "Abe Peterson," he drawled, the smile wider than ever. I'd never seen so many teeth for so long at one time in my life. Still in firm control of Pa's hand, he brought out a business card. "Sure would appreciate your vote, Mr. Washington."

Pa's cheek twitched at the mistake, but he took the card anyway.

"This your boy here?" Peterson asked.

The lawmaker's hand darted toward me. In the short time it took me to clasp it, he turned and greeted someone else. So there I stood, my hand being shaken silly by somebody making fast conversation with somebody else.

At last a voice rang out. "If y'all can find a seat, we'll get this thing started!"

Peterson edged away to the shuffling of feet. I was glad to have my hand back, even if I had to rub it to restore the feeling.

In all the milling, Shan was suddenly beside me again, her perfume once more making me as crazy as a kitten on catnip. She tugged on my arm, and my legs quivered down the aisle to the third pew from front. I let Shan scoot in next to my folks and Wally, and then I sat beside her.

I was barely aware when a local farmer introduced

Peterson to the crowd. But when the lawmaker gave him one of those joint-loosening handshakes and took the podium, I was all ears.

"Evening, friends," said Peterson, adjusting his glasses. "Sure feels good knowing y'all wanted me to come down and visit with you about the election."

Pa squirmed uncomfortably, and Wally's mustache twitched.

"I was born and raised on a little ranch out in West Texas," continued the lawmaker, "but I turned out to be a legislator. Your sons and daughters can turn out to be successful folks, too. All they need's the right people in government."

Even Ma, whose patience with a long-winded sermon in church was unmatched, shifted uneasily.

Peterson's voice rose in a crescendo which I doubt even the pastor could have matched.

"You fine folks can begin by re-electing me!"

Had there been glass windows, they surely would have rattled.

Flashing that beaming smile, the lawmaker rocked back and forth on his heels. "We need leadership, friends, the kind I've been showing for the last two years."

Little Susie yawned and pointed out the circling candlebugs to her sock doll. My thoughts began to wander, too, straight to Shan. Then the click of heels at the door brought me turning with a host of others to see a second stranger come in.

Leathery and lean, with silvery temples, the distinguished-looking man wore a big Stetson hat and cowboy boots with underslung heels. Add to this the broad silver belt buckle and gold watch fob, and he stood out among all the farmers in overalls like a heifer in a pea patch. Unabashed by the attention, he took a seat next to Sam Morgan on the back pew.

Meanwhile, Peterson rambled on, harping on his merits as a legislator. After a full forty minutes marked by Pa's squirming, Peterson was still showing that at least he had the stoutest lungs in the state. Finally Pa couldn't take anymore. Rising, he faced the lawmaker.

"Excuse me," Pa interrupted, as politely as possible.

Peterson stopped in mid-sentence and gave another broad smile. "Why, certainly, Mr. Washington."

Pa glanced around at his fellow farmers. "We been sittin' here a good while now, listenin' to how qualified you are. Well, I don't doubt that or nothin', it's just that I think it's time you got down to business."

"Yeah!" chimed in Wally. "Get down to business!"

Peterson's smile faded. He took off his horn-rimmed glasses and began cleaning them on his lapel. "I'm, uh . . . what is it I can do for you?"

One farmer, visibly irritated, jumped to his feet. "What the devil you think we wrote you to come here for?"

A true politician, Peterson kept his composure. "Why, my aides left the impression you folks were interested in the election."

"We didn't write you about no dat-blamed election!" exclaimed the irritated farmer. "We wanted to see about gettin' some help in this drouth!"

Peterson frowned. "Oh, yes, I believe my aide did mention something about that."

"Well," spoke up Wally, "can you get us any help?"

"Oh, the legislature's not in session now," Peterson said matter-of-factly.

From the back of the room came Sam Morgan's voice. "I read that Governor Ma Ferguson can call a special session anytime she gets ready."

Peterson pondered Sam's comment for a moment. "Well, if I'm re-elected, I promise that's the first thing I'll see the governor about."

"Dat-gum!" snapped Pa. "We'll all be dead by then!"

Peterson turned red and began sweating heavily. Pulling out a handkerchief, he dabbed at his forehead. "I want to help you folks, I really do."

"Then help us!" exclaimed Pa. "Go see the governor tomorrow!"

Peterson sweated and dabbed and finally got his words together. "It's not that easy. You just don't walk in on the governor. I, uh ... you, uh ... it's got to go through channels. These things take time."

Pa hung his head. "Well, time's somethin' some of us don't have much of, Mr. Peterson." His voice was that of a broken man, and I hated to hear it that way.

He was still standing there with lowered head when the lawmaker sneaked out into the night.

"Well, that's that," said Wally, rising to leave.

"Not quite," said a resonant voice from the back.

I turned to see the silver-haired stranger edge into the aisle and make his way down front. When his boot heels stopped clicking, he was standing right where Peterson had been. I watched in surprise as he pulled out a cigar and lighted it with a match he struck on his boot sole. This was a church, and nobody smoked in church, no matter what kind of meeting was going on.

"I'm C. L. Clayton," he said, dropping the burned match. "I own Diamond D Cattle Company out of Fort Worth. I intend to buy every one of you out."

A hushed murmur swept through the sanctuary.

"You what?" exclaimed Sam.

"Just what gives you the idea we're all wantin' to sell so bad?" demanded Wally.

Clayton ground the match into the floor. "I'll give every one of you twelve dollars an acre."

"Twelve dollars!" exclaimed Pa. "Well, I guess so! The land around here's worth at least twice that!"

The cattleman raised an eyebrow. "In this drouth? I don't think so."

Quiet laughter broke out from the back of the room. Everybody turned to see Sam rising to sweep a hand before him.

"Where you high-falootin' people get off comin' round here thinkin' y'all can pull somethin' off on us? We might be country, but we ain't country fools."

Clayton puffed on his cigar. "You people don't have a snowball's chance in this drouth. How many peanuts you got coming up? How much grass for your cows? How much food for your kids? What I'm giving you is a chance."

"Yeah," said Pa, the back of his neck reddening, "you come in here just like a vulture, tryin' to buy us all off at dirt-cheap prices while we all need money real bad. I'll be dat-blamed if I give my farm away to anybody."

Almost choir-like, the others voiced their agreement. But Clayton wasn't discouraged. He took a card out of his shirt pocket and handed it to the nearest farmer.

"Here's where you can reach me. I've got a feeling you'll be changing your minds before long."

Still puffing that cigar, he strode up the aisle and went out into the night.

"I'd like to know just what the devil's goin' on tonight!" exclaimed Wally. "Where'd all these turkey buzzards come from, anyway?"

Pa just stood shaking his head. Then Al Burke's voice made him turn.

"Say, what's that phone number, anyhow? Not that I'd ever sell out, just curious."

"Says 8-2901," said the farmer with the card.

I looked at Pa and saw his lips silently form those numbers.

"Since everybody else in Texas is givin' advice tonight," said Wally, "I might as well too. I read in the paper where there's a rainmaker up north of Dallas."

"Land sakes, a rainmaker!" repeated Sam. "That's gettin' pretty desperate, ain't it?"

"Way things are," said Pa, "I'll try anything."

"Luke!" chastised Ma. "That's the work of the devil!"

"I think," continued Wally, "he was chargin' fifty dollars outright and two hundred more if he makes it rain."

"Whew!" exclaimed one farmer. "That's a lot of money."

"Ain't that bad, if we was to spread it out over a bunch of families," said Wally. "What do y'all say?"

Despite Ma's objections, Pa and the others agreed to give the rainmaker a try. Shan looked at me, and I looked at her. I bet she and I were thinking the same thing. A rainmaker! Coming right here to these hills!

I wasn't about to say anything to Ma, but it all sounded pretty exciting to me. And maybe Shan would be right there with me, watching him make all that water pour down out of the sky!

Chapter 3

——⁓⁓∽⊙⊱⊙⊁⊙∽⊙⁓⁓——

Do or Die

After I finished my morning chores three days later, I donned my cap and headed for Shan's. It was the only way I knew to get my mind off our troubles. Sal followed me like a dog as far as she could. Then I cut through a dusty field, climbed the barbed wire fence, and wound through a live oak thicket. It was tangled the whole way with thorny underbrush and cut by dry, twisting creeks.

I was headed into a stiff wind, and I guess that's why the wolf didn't pick up my scent. Bursting on a small clearing in the crook of a gully, I saw a patch of fur scampering through the yellowing brush.

I stopped dead in my tracks and saw the blood and hair of a Spanish goat under an algerita bush. It was just a kid, or it had been, before the wolf had killed it and fed on it.

Shaken, I went on, but my knees quaked all the way to the Burkes'. At the gnarled live oak shading a white house with high gables and green trim, I followed the flat rocks to a breezy covered porch. My mood was somber now, but I still took off my cap and tried to slick back my hair. I sure didn't want to look like a hobo in front of Shan.

"Well, well. For somebody that's gonna be ridin' a smelly ol' horse, you sure are primpin', Josh!"

Shan was at the screen door!

I know I must have blushed. I think I must have stammered something, too, but I doubt it made sense.

She opened the screen and welcomed me with that sweet smile. "Well, don't just stand there with a dumb look on your face—come on in!"

I followed her in, glad to see her in her accustomed plaid shirt and jeans so I'd be less likely to babble like a fool. Still, those old clothes couldn't hide her charms or dull her personality. I didn't know how she had developed such a friendly approach to people or such a positive attitude. Life had sure been rough on her, a lot rougher than on me. She had been only three when her ma had died, and it had been up to Mr. Burke to be both father and mother to her.

We were in a big gray room with a fireplace and modest old furniture. As soon as I turned so that the light from the door flooded my face, Shan must have seen more than just the glazed eyes of a star-struck boy.

"Josh? Somethin' the matter?"

"Over by the creek. A wolf. It got one of your kid goats."

That contagious smile of hers faded. I knew how much she loved their animals, especially the young ones that

23

seemed so fragile. Mr. Burke even had a had time getting her to eat a beef when he slaughtered it.

"I just caught a glimpse of him," I added, "but that's what it was."

"Oh, Josh! You saw it? Be careful! Dad says rabies always gets real bad when there's a drouth on!"

I shrugged. "Looks like things just keep gettin' worse and worse."

Suddenly her eyes took on that old sparkle, and she smiled impishly. "Well, maybe not *everything*," she said, and then nudged me in the shoulder.

I wondered if I blushed again, because my mouth sure went dry. I looked down, a little shiver running through me. There was no dirt on the floor to smooth out, but I tried to anyway. When I looked up, those dancing blue eyes, rosy cheeks, and inviting lips were there to greet me. And then, for a moment so filled with opportunity, I said something really dumb.

"Wh-where's the horses at?"

She stamped her little foot. "Is that all you've got to say?"

"I, uh … you, uh …" I never knew how easy it was for my tongue to get all tangled.

"*Horses,* he says." She looked away, shaking her head. Then she turned and grabbed my arm. "Come on, then," she sighed impatiently, shoving me out the door. "*Horses!*"

Soon our mounts were nodding along through brushy mesquites that alone seemed to thrive in drouth. Shan was in the lead, her ponytail jogging to the easy gait of a leggy roan with a long mane. I was bouncing along on Donner, a big bay with lots of muscle. The brittle nubs of grass crackled under our horses' hoofs with every stride.

"Isn't the country just burned up so bad?" asked Shan. "Dad says he's never seen it in such a shape."

"What did he think of the meeting the other night?"

She pulled rein and we stopped to face each other. All of a sudden her eyes seemed awfully solemn.

"Things look pretty bad, Josh. The bank's after him about that loan he took out a couple of years back. You know, they made him put up the whole place."

"He did? We gotta scrape up some money real quick, too. I don't know what's gonna come of things."

"Dad's in town to see about gettin' hold of the stock yards in Fort Worth. He's afraid he's gonna have to sell the cows to keep our heads above water."

"But they'll go dirt cheap the way things are!"

There was a lot of emotion in Shan's eyes, and her voice choked. "He . . . he even said last night that if things don't get better, we might have to sell out."

"You . . . you'd be . . . movin'?"

Those blue eyes began to glisten, and she hung her head.

Shan leaving! No! She couldn't go, she just couldn't! Pa was going to pull us out of this fix, and Shan just couldn't move away!

She rode on and I followed, sinking a little deeper inside with every nod of Donner's head. We hadn't gone far before Shan reasserted that positive outlook of hers that made her such a delight to be around.

"That rainmaker's gonna make it rain cats and dogs—

I just know he is!" she exclaimed. "He's gonna have the creeks all runnin' and the peanut fields all sproutin' and the grass thick as can be! You and me's gonna be ridin' all summer and watchin' the cows gettin' fatter by the day!"

It sure sounded good to me, especially that part about the two of us. Now I couldn't think about drouths or banks or anything but that slight perfume of hers.

What was happening to me? Could it have been like Wally Fingers always said, in the spring a young man's fancy turns to the things girls have been thinking about all winter long?

In a small, breezy meadow in the bend of a dry creek, we dismounted. Shan sat in a patch of green rye. But I just stood there, adjusting my cap and trying to muster the nerve to join her. The timber was thick around us, a tangle of briars and gnarled grapevines twisting into the upper limbs. There were shady post oaks and rustling elms, leafy red oaks and trembling mesquites. Over at creek's edge beside our casually hitched horses, a bush bloomed red among tender-leaved live oak sprouts. It was almost as if the drouth had missed this one spot.

I heard the chatter of a squirrel, and I craned to spot it clinging to an upper oak limb.

"Looka there!" I exclaimed, pointing. But by the time Shan lifted her gaze, the squirrel had already scampered out of sight.

"What was it, Josh?" she asked, scouting the limbs.

The breeze rippled a loose lock of hair at her cheek. I watched it dance, blond against peach, and suddenly dwelled on those inviting lips. A shiver ran down my back. Could I...? Did I dare to...?

She turned and caught me staring. I must have jumped like a scared rabbit. But there we were eye to eye, a pretty girl and a weak-kneed boy.

"Wha'd you see up there?" she asked again.

"Aw, j-just an ol' squirrel."

"Isn't this place just so pretty?"

"Uh-huh, almost as ... almost as pretty as ..."

Well, I'd already started now, and figured I might as well go ahead and blurt it out.

"... as you are."

"Why, Josh!" she exclaimed with a twinkle in her eyes. "That's the first time you ever told me that!"

There was a three-foot mesquite limb beside her, but she tossed it aside to make room. "Why don't you sit down here with me?"

"I, well, I ..." I looked back up in the trees. Then she seized my hand and I turned to see her patting the grass.

"Sit *down*, will you?"

I glanced up at the limbs again. "I-I was just lookin' for that squirrel again." But I did find the courage to ease down at her side.

A little past Shan was a bouquet of yellow flowers, and she bent away to study them. "Oh, how pretty!" she said, running her fingers across the petals.

I leaned close for a look. As I did, my cheek was almost against hers, and flowers were the farthest thing from my mind.

I hadn't ever kissed a girl, but as I sat there watching

her play with those flowers, I became determined, do or die, to plant a kiss on Shan. I was glad I hadn't forgotten to brush my teeth after breakfast. Her perfume sent a thrill through me, and I edged nearer until my chest touched her shoulder. Just as I started to pucker, the most embarrassing thing in the world happened.

She turned around and the bill of my cap hit her right in the nose!

I must have looked like a catfish out of water, the way I flopped away from her. But even as I cast a look of complete embarrassment to the ground, I knew she was looking at me. She was staring, and all I could do was sit there like a big, dumb kid with his hand caught in the cookie jar.

All of a sudden I felt my cap sliding off. I looked up and found a smile lighting up her face.

"Josh, do you want to kiss me?"

I was so surprised that all I could do was whimper like a puppy dog and nod. Those eager lips widened even more in a smile, and she drew near with eyes closed. I swallowed so hard it must have sounded like ol' Sal downing her cud. I put my arm around her and my armpits suddenly felt dripping wet. Leaning close, I puckered my lips and pressed them against hers.

I didn't know what to do once I got them there, but I decided to keep them there long enough to find out. All the while, I kept my eyes open—I didn't want to miss anything. I guess my awkwardness finally got the best of her, because she was the one who finally figured out this kiss wasn't going anywhere. But at least as she withdrew she didn't let on and embarrass me further. And anyway, she was smiling.

"I was wonderin' if you were ever goin' to do that," she said, cuddling close. "I think I'm really goin' to enjoy this summer."

Boy! I thought. What a summer this was going to be!

But that was before our horses suddenly bolted free and I whirled to face a red fox, wild-eyed and frothy-mouthed as it burst out of the brush.

Chapter 4

People Around Here

"Look out!" I cried.

I knew that nothing but rabies could make a fox lose its natural fear of man. A red fox was supposed to be so shy, relying on its cunning to hunt rabbits and field mice. But this one had devil eyes fixed right on us, and through all the foam I could see plenty of long, sharp teeth.

It slung its head, flecking its rust-red coat and black stockings with froth. It was nearly three feet long from angular snout to rump, and every inch of it seemed intent on evil. Its pointed ears were erect and its back was arched, and it carried its bushy, white-tipped tail with a strange bend. It came at us sideways on stiff legs that made it all the more scary.

Shan gave a startled gasp, and then we were both on our feet. I stumbled over the thick limb and whirled left and right. We were backed against a wall of brush with no place to run!

"Josh! Josh!" cried Shan, clinging to me. "He's got rabies, Josh!"

Briars were biting into my shoulders, the crackling underbrush pushing hard against my back. I had to scare the thing away!

"Hyaah!" I shouted. "Git! Git out of here!"

But the devil fox still came sidling straight at us, its vicious teeth bared and its flanks heaving to its labored breaths.

"Git! Hyaah! Hyaah!"

There was no turning the animal! It was right on top of us, and the fever madness was in its eyes!

"Josh! Josh!" cried Shan. "He's gonna get us, Josh!"

I lunged for the mesquite limb at my feet. It was like a club as I gripped it. Fifteen pounds of sure death leaped for my throat. From a crouch, I brought the limb up like a cattle prod and caught the fox solidly in the shoulder. It fell away, but it was back on its feet in an instant and coiling itself for another spring.

I was suddenly in the batter's box in a game that meant life or death.

"Josh! Josh!" cried Shan.

"Find a tree!" I yelled.

I'd played a lot of baseball over the years, so I knew how to handle a bat. My problem had always been connecting. If I struck out this time, I knew I'd be in for a long, long sleep.

As the animal started its deadly pounce, I swung for the fences and caught it hard in the skull. I'd never known such raw power. It dropped at my feet like a second-rate fighter under the fists of Jack Dempsey. It lay there, stunned and trembling and smearing the grass with foam.

For once, I had hit a home run.

"Let's get out of here!" I cried.

We ran like startled jackrabbits. But with every stride, a single thought raced through in my mind.

I'd kissed Shan and fought for her, and now she was . . . my girlfriend!

———❦———

As the last-gasp deadline for the mortgage payment approached, Pa tried every honorable way of raising the funds. He went town to town, asking for jobs with advance pay. He bounced in and out of banks in search of another loan. He even swallowed his pride and met man to man with Mr. Hodgkins one last time. After offering the banker everything we had besides our land and each other, Pa was turned away cold. But not before he had told the newcomer a thing or two.

"You just don't understand about people around here, do you?" Pa had said with passion. "I mean the kind that grew up with this land. The kind that's carved this country out of oak thickets and rocky creeks. They's the kind of folks that's made life worth livin', even if they never had two bits their whole life. You just don't give a dat-blame about none of that, do you?"

Night after night, Pa stayed up late, looking for answers in the dog-eared pages of his Bible. But there just didn't seem to be any.

Then came that dark, uncaring day before deadline. It looked as if we had just one more night to call the place ours. Pa decided we should observe it in the same way we'd lived our lives—with faith. He called us together around the little blue table in the living room and laid his open Bible before us. The four of us sat there in cane-bottom chairs and watched the lamplight flicker on the loose pages yellowed with age. After a minute of silent reflection, Pa pushed the book across to me.

"Why don't you read the first couple of verses, Josh?"

"Sure, Pa. 'Though I speak with the tongues of men and of angels, and have not charity, I am become as sounding brass, or a tinkling cymbal. And though I have the gift of prophecy, and understand all mysteries, and all knowledge; and though I have all faith, so that I could remove mountains, and have not charity, I am nothing.'"

"What do you think Paul's tryin' to tell us here?" Pa asked.

"Don't charity mean love?" I asked. "I guess he's sayin' if you don't have love, you don't have anything."

Pa nodded and stared at the crinkled page a moment. Then he lifted his gaze to Ma. "So what's the most important thing in life?"

"Charity—love." Ma looked down and began to twirl her wedding ring. It was all she had of my grandmother's. "Even if you're king of the world, and help the poor, and even give up your life doin' it, if you didn't do it out of love, it's worthless."

Pa ran his fingers along the table. "Y'all think we've got love?"

Without hesitation, Ma reached for Pa's hand on her right and Susie's on her left. It prompted us all to join hands, an unbroken circle centered in faith.

"There's more warmth and love right here in this family," Ma said, "than I ever believed possible in the whole world."

Pa was all but overcome by emotion. "This family," he said with a tremble, "is held together by somethin' stronger than any blizzard, any flood, or any drouth. And our love will still be just as strong when those other things don't even exist no more."

I'd never felt so close to my family as in that moment. I could almost feel God's presence in our clasped hands. His Spirit seemed to fill me even more as we bowed our heads to Pa's heartfelt prayer.

"Good Lord," he began with deep reverence, "we thank You for everything we got. But most of all, Lord, we thank you for each other. Your love's made us what we are.

"Now, we think we need money real bad, but only You know whether we really ought to have it or not. No matter what, Good Lord, we ain't gonna hold it against You. There ain't nothin' can take away our love for You or each other."

We all said "Amen" and looked up, but our hands stayed clasped as if we never wanted to let go.

Chapter 5

A Black Storm

Pa was up early that final morning, making a last-ditch effort to find a job. By daybreak, he and I were speeding down dusty roads, thanks to Mr. Burke and his clattering old Ford. But times had never been this hard, and there just weren't any jobs to be had.

Pa was a broken man on the way home. His face was pale, and there were heavy bags under his glazed eyes. In a single day he had aged ten years.

When Mr. Burke sadly bid us goodbye at our gate, Sal was there to greet us and the shadows of the twin post oaks were growing long. But the darkness that choked me had nothing to do with the falling sun.

At the back door of our house, Pa hesitated and scanned the sprawling fields one last time. The blowing dust was whipping the bare rows worse than ever. Pa's crow's-footed eyes began to glisten, and I wanted so much to help him. But all I could do was reach over and take his hand.

He turned to me, and his chin began to quiver. He tried to say something, but the words just wouldn't come. Then he pulled me close and we just stood there, a boy and his father needing each other so very, very much.

We went inside and found Ma sweeping the kitchen. She spoke Pa's name, but he went straight to the table, threw down his hat, and sank into a chair.

"Ain't no use in you sweepin' out the kitchen," he whispered, hanging his head. "It ain't gonna be ours no more."

Ma went to his side and put her left hand on his shoulder. "Darlin', oh, darlin'."

"It's all over, Sarah. All over."

"No, it's not, Luke. It's not. Things are in the Lord's hands, not nobody else's."

I thought she was just trying to comfort him, and so did he. He reached up and laid his browned hand on hers, so that both rested on his shoulder. As he gently stroked her fingers, his eyes suddenly widened and he looked puzzled. He turned to Ma's hand and then to her smiling face.

Her wedding ring was gone.

"I went to town today," she said softly. "I made that payment—and the one after it—with my ring."

Pa just went blank. Then it sank in, and I'd never seen such surprise, relief, and love fill anyone's eyes before. Scooting back his chair, he stood and looked into Ma's beautiful, smiling face.

"Sarah! Sarah, it was your ma's!"

She just pulled him close, and I joined them in a bond of love. But even as I did, a dark thought filled my mind. How could we ever meet the payments to come?

———⟿⟋⟍⟋⟍⟋⟍⟋⟍⟿———

The days that followed brought no rain, just barren skies with a branding-fire sun. The water in the cow trough almost boiled, and even the mesquite leaves began to yellow and curl. I'd never seen a spring so scorching.

Every afternoon I'd try to make it over to see Shan. The only difference now was that I always carried a .410 shotgun and traveled the lane. Ever since the fox incident, Ma and Pa insisted on it.

For the most part, Shan and I stayed around her house. Neither of us was anxious to meet up with another rabid animal. But when her dad was around and we wanted some time to ourselves, we'd slip out to the porch. I still hadn't gotten the hang of this lip-lock business, but Shan was swell enough to put up with me.

A couple of weeks after the Hilldale meeting, I went out our kitchen door and started for the garden in back of the windmill. Pa had screwed a hose on the stand pipe faucet, and he stood squirting water on the parched tomato plants. As I passed the parked wagon, I saw Susie through the spokes of the front wheel. She was sitting under the wagon bed, playing with her sock doll and scratching in the dirt.

"Ma's gonna skin you alive if you come in all dirty," I warned as I passed.

Just as I reached the gnarled old mesquite where the chickens liked to roost, I caught the threatening sky through the skeleton of the mill. Here, the sun beat down out of a cloudless blue. But sweeping all the way across the northern horizon was a dark, reddish-brown cloud. It seemed to be rising before my very eyes.

As I neared the garden, I could see a rainbow in the spray Pa sent falling across the neat rows of wilted vegetables. But this rainbow didn't mean rain.

"Look at the duster we got comin', Pa," I said.

He took his finger off the nozzle and lifted his gaze. What he saw was enough to cause the hose to slip from his fingers. The cloud was fast becoming a black, swirling devil. It was choking the life from the sky as it rolled in over barren fields and tangled thickets. It was boiling and churning and bearing down on us mighty fast.

From where I was, Pa appeared framed against that storm. He was just a single frail man, and yet he stood there for the longest time and stared, as if he could somehow make that cloud go away.

"Pa? Pa, it's just a dust storm, sand and stuff."

I took his arm, suddenly lost in worry about him. When he looked at me, I'd never seen quite the same fear in his eyes before.

"It ain't just that, Josh. It's . . ." His voice choked, and he swept a hand toward the bare fields. "It's everything. It's got us licked, and there ain't nothin' we can do about it. I can look up there at that storm and tell that."

I found a knot in my throat as I tugged on his arm. "Come on in, Pa. It's gonna be a booger. Come on in."

He glanced skyward one last time and then hung his head and went with me.

Ma was stoking the wood-burning cookstove when we reached the house. I closed the wooden door behind us and she looked up.

"How come you shuttin' the door, Josh?" she asked. "This stove's gonna have the whole house roastin' in a minute."

Pa tossed his sweaty hat on the table. "Got a storm comin'."

Ma straightened anxiously. *"Rain, Luke?"*

"Just the blackest-lookin' dust storm I ever seen."

Ma went to the window box and studied the sky as she pulled in the milk crock. The sky was even darker than before. "Why, it almost looks like the way I always pictured the end of the world," she said with awe.

She lowered the window and the storm struck with a fury. It peppered the glass and shook the whole window frame. Then the door flew open and a blast of wind stronger than a blue norther came barreling through the house.

"Land sakes!" cried Ma. "Get that door shut!"

Stinging grains of sand caught me in the face as I lunged for the door. Even after I seized it, it was like pushing against a stubborn mule. Then Pa threw his shoulder into it and we managed to force it shut. Even through the three-quarter-inch plywood, I could hear the gloomy howl and feel the rattle of the banging screen.

Pa lodged a chair under the doorknob and hurried away with Ma to close the other windows. I guess I should have helped too, but something about the storm drew me to the window box. The wind was whistling through a crack in the pane. Outside, the blast whipped the trees without mercy, bending the slender ones nearly double. The whirring windmill fan locked in place to weather the onslaught, but the whole mill tower seemed to sway. Within seconds, a grim darkness swept over the land. It was suddenly midnight right in the middle of afternoon.

"Susie! Where's Susie!"

Ma's frantic cry brought me whirling, but everything was pitch-black around me. Then a match ignited, a hand lighted a kerosene lamp, and I could see the panic in Ma's face.

"Josh! You seen Susie? Tell me you seen her somewhere!"

All of a sudden I was as panicked as Ma. I *had* seen Susie, and I couldn't believe I'd forgotten about her in all my worry about Pa.

I bolted. Hurling aside the lodged chair, I flung the door open and the storm roared in again.

"Susie! Susie! You hear me, Susie?"

I couldn't even hear my own voice. But I could imagine Sue-Sue's terrified cries. Throwing a shielding forearm to my eyes, I ran into the shrieking blast.

I couldn't see a thing, but I could feel plenty as I stumbled and reeled straight into the teeth of a black blizzard. The flying sand thrashed me, clawing my cheeks and raking my arms. The whip of my loose pants stung my legs, and my flailing shirttail lashed my back. I could taste the bitter dirt and winced to all the grit in my eyes.

But no matter how tough it was on me, I knew it was a hundred times worse on Sue-Sue.

I called her name again and again as I fought my way through the blinding storm. The wagon! Where was the wagon!

Something big and shadowy flew by and crashed against the house. Then came another and another, clanging as they struck. All of a sudden I realized the wind was lifting the tin roof off the barn. If one of those sharp pieces was to hit me or Susie, it could take our heads off!

Chapter 6

The Rainmaker

Suddenly I stumbled hard into something. Sweeping my hand across it, I felt the bite of splinters. It had to be the wagon!

"Susie! Susie! You here, Susie?"

Even if she'd been right in front of my face, I couldn't have heard her.

Still, I cried her name as I felt my way along the planks. The wagon was rocking wildly. I found a wheel and felt it jump, and jump again. The storm was lifting the whole vehicle! If it turned over, it was sure to crush anything under it!

All of a sudden another shadow came flying at me. I dodged, but this time it caught me hard in the shoulder and knocked me to the ground. The next thing I knew I was rolling and spinning crazily, a mere toy in a powerful wind. I yelled out and clawed at the ground and finally regained control. But when I came to my hands and knees, I didn't know left from right anymore.

I'd lost the wagon!

Then I heard the *thuh-dump! thuh-dump!* of a pitching wheel and found spokes in my face. In my wild tumble, I'd come close to getting thrown right under it. Then another dark shadow banged against the wagon and sailed overhead. I had to stay down!

But that didn't mean I'd given up. I gauged the pounding wheel's location and rolled under the wagon bed.

Here at ground level, the hurtling sand was even more punishing. It clogged my sinuses and choked my throat, and I started to panic. I couldn't breathe! It was wrenching the life right out of me! But I kept up my frantic cries as I groped in the dark.

Suddenly I squeezed something small and soft, and it squeezed back. Another instant and I was cradling Susie and her homemade doll in my arms and shielding her body with mine.

"I got you, Sue-Sue! I got you!"

We huddled there, listening to the deadly tin batter the planks about us and wrap around the far wheels. The bed was bouncing right over our heads, the wheels pounding the turf first here, then there. Those irons were doing their best to pin us!

Finally, the worst was over. The wagon grew still and the tin stopped flying. There was still plenty of wind and hanging dust, all right. But now I could see Susie's beautiful little face, and she was okay.

But was anything else?

I was still spitting dirt two days later when the four of us headed for the Burkes' in a wagon more rickety than ever. From there, we'd turn around and go into Pettit, where the rainmaker had set up the evening before.

"The very idea, Luke! A rainmaker!" Ma complained as the wagon rumbled along. "It's just not a Christianly thing!"

"And starvin' *is*?" asked Pa.

Ma's opinion wasn't going to be swayed so easily. Her life was rooted in the Good Book, and she was mighty stubborn where that was concerned.

"The only one who can make rain is the Good Lord Himself!" she went on. "Hirin' a rainmaker's nothin' but the work of Satan!"

"You want us to just sit around here with all them bare fields blowin' dust?"

"At least we don't have to bring *more* evil on ourselves!" she argued. "The Bible says, 'Thou shalt not suffer a witch to live,' and bringin' in somebody like that ain't nothing but dabblin' in witchcraft!"

Pa inhaled deeply. "I tell you what, Sarah, this rainmaker's about our last straw. We can't afford another week without rain. If somethin' big don't happen quick, our crops won't make again and we'll have to sell them cows for little of nothin'."

I cringed at the thought of selling ol' Sal. She was my pet!

"And don't forget," Pa added, "we got another payment to make—and you ain't got no more rings to pay it with."

I straightened. "You really think that man can make it rain, Pa?"

He shrugged. "There's a lot of things I don't know. But the Lord gives different gifts of the spirit to different people. Paul says so in First Corinthians."

"Still," contended Ma, "why trust in man when the only One you can depend on is God?"

"But the Good Lord works *through* man, Sarah. You know that."

I turned to the parched and dusty fields that ached for rain and wished I were as sure as Pa.

We picked Shan up, and then we were off for town. I think Ma and Pa were as glad as I was to have her along. The two of them were at odds right now, and with a guest present they'd keep their opinions to themselves and maybe cool off a bit. I sure hoped so.

All the way to Pettit the road bled dusty to the hoofs of the mules. On both sides, the land stretched, burned and shriveled, to faraway hills that danced gray in the shimmering heat waves. We pulled up in front of the general store, where Sam Morgan sat on the porch, smoking his pipe.

"Mornin', Sam," said Pa, keeping his seat in the wagon. "Say, that rainmaker hit town?"

"Well, howdy, folks. Yeah, he's here, and dat-blamed if I ever saw anything like it."

"He started tryin' to make it rain yet, Mr. Morgan?" asked Shan. "I just know he'll do it!"

"Wain! Wain!" cried Sue-Sue.

Sam half-laughed. "You'll just have to see for yourself,

hon. I couldn't describe the goings-on." Then he looked at Pa and his expression turned solemn. "I just hope this ain't for nothin', Luke."

Pa bit his lower lip. "I'm prayin' the same thing, Sam. Mighty hard."

Sam pointed us west of town, and soon we burst on a sight to behold. On the right was a big, vacant lot with plenty of broomweeds and clinging tatters of paper. Jamming that acre were dozens of people. They milled like nervous cattle, gabbing and craning and staring. Their children ran and played around the cars and wagons that spilled out on both sides of the lane.

Pa raised an eyebrow. "Whew! That feller might not've brought no rain yet, but he durned sure brought the people."

He looked at Ma, but I don't think he liked the look she gave him back.

Pa parked under a left-side post oak with bare, spidery limbs. I jumped off first and gave Shan a helping hand down. She didn't let go, and I didn't, either. Boy! What a tremor passed through me as we crossed the lane hand in hand and squeezed through all the cars!

Pushing through the stirring crowd, I caught a glimpse of something that brought me to tiptoes for a better look. It was a wagon with a high wooden side and red, white, and blue stripes. Bold black letters across the middle spelled out the words "Samford Allred, Rainmaker."

The paint was chipped and peeling, and the wagon irons were awfully rusty. I hoped it was a sign the rig spent a lot of time out in the rain. The mules certainly made a fellow think that way, for their big ears stuck up through rubber rain hoods of bright yellow. I knew now what Sam Morgan had meant.

The crowd pushed forward and carried us with it. Everybody's attention seemed fixed on something near the rear of the wagon. My view was still blocked, but I could smell wood smoke and see it spiral up.

"What do you see, Josh? What do you see?" asked Shan, craning for a glimpse.

About that time I bumped into Wally Fingers.

"Howdy there, Josh!" His handlebar mustache twitched. "Where's your pa at?"

"Hi, Wally. Somewhere around here. Say, what's goin' on over there? I ain't tall enough to see."

Wally stretched his full six feet two inches and peered over the hat of the man in front of us. "Look's like the rain-maker's about to do his stuff!"

I led Shan on through until we had a clear view. Thirty feet behind the wagon, smoke rose from a fire that lapped a big sooty pot like the one Ma did her washing in. The vehicle's rear doors were ajar, and there was a man leaning inside, rummaging among jars and old apple crates.

Shan pressed close to me, and I didn't mind a bit. "That wagon of his is funny enough, but look at that get-up of his, Josh!"

The man brought out a tin lid, and I had a good look at him. He was a shriveled little fellow in a fireman's hat and a yellow rain slicker with his name on back. His bristly face was thin and drawn, with a lower jaw that stuck out oddly. When he started for the fire, he had a kink in his gait. As he added wood, bystanders grilled him with questions. But

47

he just smiled, showing teeth like broken fence slats, and went about his work.

Soon Allred had a roaring fire. I could hear it crackle and pop as the yellow flames lapped the stewer. He fitted the lid on top and then limped to the wagon. This time he came out with several bottles of orange, blue, and yellow powders.

We stood like charmed animals as he went back to the fire and, with pliers, lifted the lid to bring steam rising. Adding the powders to the boiling water, he stood as straight as his stooped shoulders would allow and motioned us back.

"Please, just a little ways," he urged in a squeaky voice.

Slowly, we all retreated with a lot of jostling. The people in back didn't want to give ground.

"Appreciate it," said Allred with a snaggletoothed smile. "Can't be responsible for accidents." Pulling a flask out from under his slicker, he poured a little into the brew and then took a swig himself. Replacing the lid, he backed away.

I watched with growing fascination as the lid began to bounce like a frisky calf.

"Oh, I'm so excited!" exclaimed Shan. "He's really gonna do it, Josh!"

A minute passed, and then two. By now the lid was really dancing. Still, Allred added wood, until I could barely see the pot for all the flames. Tossing in one last log, the rainmaker rushed away and crouched behind a wagon wheel.

"It's comin'!" he yelled.

I looked up, thinking he meant rain, but the sky was as

bare as our fields. When I lowered my gaze, the whole stewer had disappeared in the bonfire. But I could still hear the gurgle of the brew and clatter of the lid.

Ka-boom!

There was an abrupt explosion like both barrels of Pa's shotgun going off. A hot blast hit me and a big orange cloud was suddenly all around. I caught a glimpse of the lid forty feet in the air, and then *nobody* waited to see what happened next! As a dozen mules snorted and reared in their harnesses, we bolted from the fire. I'd never seen so many people scatter so fast.

As the jumble of parked vehicles stopped everybody's flight, I turned to see the rainmaker standing calmly at his wagon. Now I saw that his slicker wasn't such a bad idea, considering how the brew had flown in every direction. Meanwhile, the fire was still belching that orange cloud.

All of a sudden everybody was talking at once.

"What the devil's he doin'?" exclaimed Wally. "Tryin' to kill us all?"

"Rainmaker!" cried another. "Why, if that lid had hit somebody, they'd never need no more water of *any* kind!"

Beside me, Shan was giggling.

"What's the matter?" I asked.

"Oh, nothin' much," she said, a sparkle in her eyes. "Except you sure look funny with orange dust all over your face!"

I raised an eyebrow. "Oh, is that right? Well, I bet my face don't look half as funny as that orange mug *you* got!"

She gasped, wiping her cheek and inspecting her tinged fingers. But that smile of hers stayed as sweet as ever.

Then I turned and saw Pa nearby. He seemed so alone as he lifted his weary face to that manmade cloud spreading across the sky. He just stood there and stared, and then Ma came up with Susie and put a comforting arm around him.

"Ladies! Gentlemen! If you'll step right up here . . . !"

I turned to that colorful wagon and saw the rainmaker standing before it. He held up a flask and waved it like a regular showman.

"Good folks!" he shouted. "I won't be breaking open the sky again till later, so meantime let me show you something! This bottle here is special vitamin water you can't buy in any store! For two bits, it'll keep arthritis down, get rid of sour stomach, even clear up your sinuses!"

Pa said something under his breath, and I turned to see him roll his eyes. But Wally, standing right in front of me, was more vocal. He let loose a couple of choice words he normally wouldn't have used around women or youngsters.

I looked at Shan, my spirits slipping. "I think I'm gonna be sick."

"The way *he* talks, he's got the cure!"

"You a rainmaker or a tonic salesman?" an agitated Wally demanded of Allred.

"Never hurts to be diversified! Can I fix you up with a bottle, mister?"

I felt a tap on my shoulder. "Let's get out of here!" snapped Pa, starting for the wagon without waiting for us.

On the way home we were a pretty glum bunch. Pa had just given Wally about our last dollar for our share of the cost, and it had bought us admission to a medicine show. Pa was silent until the big post oaks fronting our farm came in sight. Then, Shan or no Shan, he turned to Ma and spoke his mind.

"Well, go ahead and say it."

"Say what?"

"Say, *I told you so.*"

"Luke! You know I'd never do that!"

"Just the same, that's what you're thinkin'."

"No, it's not! The only thing I'm doin' is prayin' the Lord will help us!"

I knew Pa was really feeling low, so I groped for something to say. "Can't judge that rainmaker by one look, Pa."

"He'll make it rain, Mr. Watson!" spoke up Shan. "He's just got to!"

Pa didn't respond, and I couldn't blame him. I knew we were thinking the same thing.

That man couldn't make it rain if he had a hundred years to try.

My folks got off at the gate, and I took Shan home in the wagon. When I pulled up under the big oak at her house, I mustered all my courage.

"Shan? Uh, there's gonna be a, uh . . . a dance Saturday week at the Maynard barn."

Her eyes lighted up. "Oh?"

"Uh-huh." I looked down and fumbled with the reins. "I don't suppose you'd, uh . . . you'd want to go."

"Of course I would, Josh!"

I was going to my first dance, and Shan was going with me!

Chapter 7

Hydrophobia

The day after we fed the cows our last bale of hay, Pa and I stood at a sun-baked peanut field. The rows held nothing but swirling sand that rasped against our legs.

"Even if it was to rain ten inches 'fore sundown," he said, "this stuff'd still never make."

"Pa, what's gonna happen to our cows, to ... Sal?"

He lifted his gaze to our dusty pasture and squinted to the glare. "We're gonna have to just flat *give* them away, Josh."

I shuddered. I knew it would kill me to part with that motley-faced old cow. She was a pet, as much as any dog would have been. How could we just shuffle her off that way?

"Give the rainmaker a chance, Pa," I pleaded. "He's just been here a few days."

Suddenly Pa's face showed all kinds of impatience. "In

a few *more* days all them cows'll be dead. Is that what you want?"

A grim silence fell over us, but inside me the turmoil was anything but hushed.

Wally Fingers dropped by that evening and we learned some disturbing news. Al Burke was in such a fix that he had arranged for a truck to pick up his cows the next day. He was shipping them by rail to Fort Worth to sell for whatever they'd bring.

"They'll go dirt cheap the way things are," Pa said sadly. Then he breathed sharply. "Dat-blame it all! The whole world's against us!" He lowered his head, and defeat filled his voice. "Al ain't got no choice—just like me. I'll pay him a visit and have that truck pick up my knotty ol' things while they're at it."

I broke out in a chill that wouldn't go away. We were selling Sal!

The next morning broke hotter than ever. I lay in bed for the longest, watching the dust float through a sun ray. I didn't want to face the day, but finally I forced myself up and went down to the kitchen.

Ma was sweeping behind the wood bin, the broom straws rasping against the floor.

"Thought you was gonna sleep all mornin', Josh. Bacon's on the stove and biscuits are in the oven."

I didn't have an appetite. "Where's Pa at?"

"Callin' up the cows."

I went to the screen door and saw Sal and the other cattle wandering in from the brushy creek. Around them the sun bore down, bright and steaming, just as it had my whole life. The sun had always won here, Grandpa had told me once. Soon, I feared, it would win out over us, too.

I suddenly felt Ma's touch. "You know we got to, darlin'. We can't just let Sal starve."

I wouldn't face her. But she must have sensed all the frustration and anger bottled up inside me.

"Your pa's doin' what he thinks best for us, Josh. He always has. If he thinks there ain't no way we can make it on this farm without sellin' them cows, then I know he's right."

I whirled and all my hurt spilled out. "How come we don't just leave, then? We don't have to stay here and die!"

Ma studied me solemnly. "You really mean that, darlin'? You think you could ever be happy anywhere else?"

"Well, I'm sure not happy *here!*"

I burst out the back door and headed for the pens. I could see Pa through the supports of the wooden tank tower. He had his foot propped up on the open pen gate as the cows and calves ambled in, hungry and mooing. I don't think I'd ever seen Sal so thin and drawn.

Pa closed the creaking gate and fastened it with baling wire. Leaning his forearms on the fence, he stood there and stared at the cattle. He never saw me until I propped my foot up next to his.

"I hate doin' them this way," he said, watching the stock mill and bawl. "I hate callin' them up and not havin' nothin' to feed them."

"Pa? Do we have to?"

He nodded to the bony cattle. "Look at them, Josh. You know we can't wait no longer."

"But what if we just sold part of them? Wouldn't there be enough grass just for one? Just for . . . Sal?"

Pa rasped a hand across his weary face. "We ain't got a sprig of grass on this whole place. There ain't nothin' could scrounge up enough to eat like it is. We just gotta sell them all, Josh."

Pouting, I climbed the rickety fence and went straight to Sal. The sunlight glinted on her reddish coat. She lifted her head and looked at me as I rubbed her curly poll. She twitched her big red ears, shaking the flies away, and swished her matted tail. Kneeling, I put an arm around her neck and rubbed her thick brisket. In return she lowed quietly and began chewing her cud.

"Sal, good ol' Sal," I whispered.

She nuzzled my arm, and I looked along her protruding rib cage and met Pa's gaze. Suddenly I directed all my frustration at him alone. It was *his* fault! He was the one getting rid of Sal, and he just didn't care if it hurt me or not!

As I glared at him, it was the first time I'd ever seen such shock, concern, and hurt fill his face.

"Josh, I— "

We both turned at a screeching of brakes on the lane. A big cattle truck was framed between the post oaks at the gate. I glared again at Pa, who seemed unable to find words. With a parting hug for Sal, I turned my back on my dad and climbed the side fence.

I figured I'd hurt Pa, but right then I didn't care. I

grabbed the shotgun out of the roofless barn and began walking blindly toward the creek.

I hardly knew when I crossed its cracked bed, and the ensuing rasp of crisp broomweeds against my legs came like a dream. Even the sting of blowing sand in my face couldn't erase the image of one bony old cow from my mind.

Finally I found myself deep in the back thicket. There was an oak-fringed draw here, tangled by underbrush and carpeted by fallen leaves. Fronting it was a park-like area with scattered clumps of young live oaks. I sat down on a termite-infested log and poked at a hollowed-out armadillo shell with the shotgun barrel. I toyed with it for five minutes or five hours; I didn't count.

Then I heard the bark of a squirrel high in an oak. I'd glimpsed one that day at Shan's, all right, but I hadn't seen one on our place since winter. It was as if they'd all taken up and left—or died—because of the drouth.

As I watched the critter scamper through the limbs, I saw that it was just about the scrawniest squirrel I'd ever come across. It was nothing but fur stretched over bones. Oddly, it reminded me of my family.

That stubborn old squirrel had clung to this land, only to waste away. And here the four of us were, without any more sense than to do just the same.

The wind shifted and a pungent odor singed my nostrils. I knew it immediately for what it was—a skunk. But skunks didn't usually prowl in daytime, and dusk was still hours away. Given my experience with the fox, I was glad I had a shotgun in my hands and a spare shell in my shirt pocket.

Skunks were even worse than foxes about carrying rabies, which some folks in these parts called "hydrophobia."

I whirled and saw the skunk emerge from the brush twenty feet away. It was the size of a big house cat. Its back was arched, and it carried its fluffy tail erect. Even though I was downwind, it had to know I was there. Yet it showed no fear as it rushed straight toward me on its short legs.

Hydrophobia!

It was happening again! And this one didn't have to bite! I figured it could spray that awful disease from ten feet away!

I jumped up and threw the butt of the shotgun against my shoulder. It was a single-shot breechloader with a load already in the chamber. Maybe I could have outrun the skunk, and maybe not. But I was angry. I was sick of this whole drouth, and past the knob sight of that barrel was one more thing that life was trying to throw at me right now. I *wanted* to shoot. For weeks everything had been out of my control. Now I had things in *my* hands.

But what I didn't have were nerves of steel, not when a mad skunk was bearing down on me.

I yanked the trigger instead of squeezing. The shotgun boomed and recoiled into my shoulder. Dirt peppered the skunk's small head, and it charged on.

I cried out and whirled to run. As I did, my boot tangled in the armadillo shell and I went down hard.

Chapter 8

Thunderhead

I broke open my shotgun, and the spent load ejected with the smell of gun smoke. I fumbled for the shell in my pocket and slammed it into the chamber. I rocked back up to my elbows and saw the onrushing skunk and its sharp little teeth framed by my uplifted legs. I snapped the breechloader in place and knew there wasn't time to aim. The animal was right at my boots!

I dropped the barrel between my knees and fanned the hammer with my thumb. *Boom!* The recoil slammed me back against the ground, but the point-blank blast drove the skunk back as if it had been yanked by a rope.

I'd killed it! But that didn't keep me from scrambling to my feet with a cry and running like crazy. I ran with heaving lungs through clawing briars and thorny under-brush until I burst on our back fence and the clearing beyond.

As I looked past the rusty barbed wire, I saw something I couldn't believe. It was a rising thunderhead, blue-black with the promise of rain.

Stunned, I just stood there, watching it climb up through the sky. Rain! Rain was coming!

Whirling, I ran all the way to the main creek. Suddenly the mockingbirds seemed to sing so happily. The air tasted so sweet. A thunderhead was chasing me!

I couldn't wait to see the expression on Pa's face. We were going to have crops and grass and wouldn't have to sell ol' Sal!

Then I broke upon the last peanut field with its clear view of the pens and stopped as if I'd run into a brick wall.

The cows were gone.

I'd been so caught up in my hurt, time had lost all meaning. For all I knew, hours could have passed. And now it was too late.

The false hope made my frustration and anger ten times worse, and an awful thought suddenly darkened my whole life. *All this is Pa's fault! He doesn't care if I'm happy or not, and I don't care about him!*

The thought passed quickly, but sudden guilt took its place. How could I even *think* such a thing?

I forced myself on past the dusty field. When I reached the screeching windmill, I noticed the wagon gone. I went on in the house and found Ma writing a letter at the kitchen table. She looked up at the creak of the door spring.

"Where on earth you been, Josh? What you been shootin' at?"

"Where's Pa?" My voice was lifeless.

"He kept out one calf. He's gone over to Wally Fingers' to slaughter it. He was wantin' you to go with him."

I nodded to the screen door. "Look outside."

She looked puzzled. "What is it?" she asked, scooting back her chair and rising.

I stepped away from the door and she looked out at the sky. "Why, it's a rain cloud!"

I had never seen her so excited. She pushed open the door and ran outside. I leaned the shotgun in the corner and followed, suddenly caught up in her excitement. Dark clouds swirled overhead. We stared up as they blotted out the sun and sent a heavy shadow across the land. Lightning cracked, and I felt the ground shake with the long rumble of thunder. Rain! It was really going to rain!

A drop hit me in the face. The air suddenly had the fresh taste that only a spring shower can bring. A second drop hit my cheek, then a third. I looked over and saw Ma's smiling face raised to the sky. But her crow's-footed eyes seemed to look far past those clouds. Her lips moved silently as tears rolled down her cheeks. Then came a flash of lightning and boom of thunder and her tears were washed away.

It was raining!

Ma turned and hugged me as the raindrops soaked my back. We withdrew to hold each other at arm's length and find each other's eyes, then lifted our gazes to the sky again. It didn't matter that the drops fell so hard they stung our faces. It was raining and we had to see!

All of a sudden, to another roar of thunder that rattled the windows behind us, the rain stopped. It was as quick and complete as if somebody had shut off a valve.

Our hands slipped from each other's shoulders. We looked at the black clouds sweeping overhead and then at each other. Ma's happy smile sagged into lines of worry. It just seemed impossible for us to stand there with glistening skin, dripping hair, and mud-splattered legs and face the truth.

Drouth still had us by the throat.

"It'll start up again, Ma," I said. But as we studied the sky for a minute, then ten, the sun broke through as swollen and hot as ever.

Finally Ma let out a long sigh. "Well, at least we know there's such a *thing* as rain left in this world. But I sure wish the Lord had seen fit to let it pour."

I didn't know how much more I could take. The sky had baited and teased and promised—and then denied.

"We ain't got a chance here—Pa knows it," I snapped, emotion wrenching my voice. "It ain't gonna rain, not ever. We're just gonna sit here and die!"

Ma put her hand on my shoulder. "Life's a hard thing, Josh. Sometimes you just got to roll with the punches. Your pa worked hard with your grandpa to make this place what it is. You *really* want us to leave?"

I thought of Sal, jostled in some cattle car as it barreled down the railroad track. "I wouldn't care if I *never* saw this farm again!"

Upon Pa's return, we greeted each other as always, but now, somehow, things were different. As supper neared, Ma sent me to the garden for squash. I picked a handful from wilted vines overrun with bugs and washed it at the windmill. As I started to mount the back doorstep, I heard Ma bring up my name. I knew I was wrong in doing so, but I quickly stepped to the side and listened.

"Leave?" Pa said. "He never did tell *me* that."

"It's the drouth, Luke. It's destroyin' us all. You know what he thought of that ol' cow."

"Yeah, I know exactly how he feels. I ain't been able to think all day."

A long silence followed. I was about to go inside when Pa spoke up again.

"I just don't know what's gonna come of things, Sarah. Maybe Josh is right. Maybe we *oughta* leave."

"Oh, darlin'! This place has been in your family for so long! I don't know if we could ever be happy anywhere else!"

Pa exhaled sharply. "Josh done told you he wasn't happy *here* no more. He done told you that."

I swallowed hard.

The conflict between Pa and me hung over us at supper like a dark cloud. Neither of us mentioned Sal or the drouth or the teasing rain. But after the dishes were done, I joined him on the front porch.

He sat leaned against a pillar and whittled on a mesquite stick. With each stroke of his rusty pocketknife, a shaving fell to the pile under his upraised knee.

"You think the best thing for us to do is leave, Josh?" he asked quietly without looking up.

I hung my head and wished he hadn't asked. "I . . . I don't know, Pa," I said, barely above a whisper. "Things . . . things just ain't the same anymore."

I lifted my gaze and saw the shavings fly from Pa's knife with greater fury.

"Well, you're right about that," he said, obviously irritated. "Things *ain't* the same no more."

But they had to be! They just had to! I was turning fifteen Saturday, I was taking my girl to a dance, and I couldn't let anything spoil it!

Chapter 9

Kickin' Mule

Saturday came, a bright day among a lot of gloomy ones. Once Pa found I was celebrating my birthday by taking Shan to the dance, he took a lot of interest. We seemed close to rekindling the warmth that had been missing between us for days now.

"Yes, sir," he told me on the front porch as he cut my hair, "if I was a young man again, that Shannon Burke would be the one I'd chase after, too."

When Susie saw me decked out in my Sunday best that evening, it was all Ma could do to keep her from climbing in the wagon with her button-eyed doll.

"I go, Joss. I go," she kept saying.

Finally I picked her up and told her that if she'd stay, I'd learn some new songs at the dance to sing for her.

As I drove the wagon out the gate, the lane was as powdery as ever. Still, all I could do was smile. Finally, the tension between Pa and me had eased a little, and I was taking a girl to my first dance. All the way up the lane, I sang a Jimmie Rodgers song I'd heard on our wind-up Victrola. It was "You and My Old Guitar," but I'd renamed it "Shan and My Old Guitar."

Things were looking up.

When Shan came out of her house, my jaw dropped. She looked so grown-up! She had on a pink dress and a belt with dangling charms. Her shoes were pearly, and tiny gold earrings danced against her cheeks. And that blond hair of hers! The ponytail had given way to flowing tresses!

We were already a mile down the lane before I noticed something else. She was awfully quiet, and her eyes looked sad. And was that a quiver in her chin, even when she tried to smile?

"Hey, somethin' the matter tonight?" I asked over the clomp of the mules' hoofs. "You're sure not talkin' much."

She smiled weakly. "Does that mean I usually do?"

"Come on, what's ailin' you?"

She glanced down. "I . . . I'm just so scared, Josh. So scared about everything."

"What do you—"

"Let's just go have the best time we ever had!" she exclaimed, as bubbly as ever. She scooted close and cuddled. "Let's have fun and not worry about anything else! What was that song you was singin' when you pulled up? Your ol' guitar and *who*?"

It was a good thing I couldn't see myself in a mirror. My face must have turned as red as a beet. But at least Shan was giggling now.

Even before we pulled up to the Maynard barn, we could hear a guitar chording to the lightning-fast notes of a mandolin. Set in a grove of oaks away from the road, the barn was one of the few around with a wooden floor and electricity. Under open rafters, square dancers stepped to the calls of Stanley Allsup, the old barber from Pettit. He stood with fiddle under chin, brushing away the straw that drifted down from the hayloft.

We walked in holding hands, and was I proud when everybody looked around at us! For a couple of minutes, we mingled with neighbors and a few visitors from Indian Gap. One young fellow sure seemed to have eyes for Shan, and I didn't like it. He followed us to the lemonade bucket, flirting with her. Before I could pick up a fruit jar, he was already filling one.

"Here, honey, let *me* get it for you," he insisted.

She accepted with a warm "Thanks!," and I was so shaken I forget to pour myself any.

Was I that far gone? Jealous just because some other boy spoke to her?

We danced to a lot of songs that night, and I'd never felt so happy. I was nervous at first—Ma had warned me not to step on Shan's toes—and I held her as far away as I could. But watching how Wally Fingers swung the ladies to his loud "Ahh-haa!," I gained enough confidence to pull her close during the waltzes. Finally, after a lively hoedown, I led her off the dance floor.

"I'm plumb wore out!" I panted.

"*You're* tired!" she exclaimed. "I'd've keeled over twenty minutes ago if you hadn't been holdin' me up!"

That smile of hers had never looked so sweet.

I nodded to the burlap sacks of feed against the wall. "Why don't you go over yonder and sit? I'll get us something to drink."

I crossed to the lemonade bucket and reached for a fruit jar. Wally came up, his handlebar mustache twitching. He glanced at Shan and grinned at me.

"Sure wish *I* was fifteen again, Josh ol' boy! You taken her out in the dark yet and whispered in her ear?"

"Whispered what, Wally?"

He punched me playfully. "You know, some of them *I love you's.*"

I guess I turned plenty red. "Oh, Wally," I said, snickering.

"Go on! That ear of hers is just a-waitin'!"

As I began filling a jar, I looked at Shan and started to wonder. I guess I poured and wondered too long, because lemonade suddenly went everywhere.

"Whoa!" exclaimed Wally. "Say, you better run whisper in that little girl's ear before you drown us all!"

He egged me on for another minute or two before I spotted Shan over with the musicians. Mr. Allsup, fiddle in hand, was bent low to make out her words above the mandolin picking. He nodded and their talk ended. I slipped free of Wally and met her at the feed sacks.

"What was that all about?" I asked as we sat.

"Oh, nothin'. What was you and Wally up to?"

"Oh, I, uh ... he, uh ..." That ear of hers sure looked inviting, all right.

"You, uh, he, uh ... *what?*" she teased.

The music stopped with a long note dragged by the fiddle bow. "I, uh ... uh ... Wanna give her a go next song?"

Her cheeks dimpled. "Let's wait a bit. They got a special singer comin' up."

"Oh?" I glanced over and saw only the musicians. "Who's that?"

"Shh! They're fixin' to announce him now."

Mr. Allsup stepped forward and lifted his bow. "We're real fortunate to have us a special singer here tonight, somebody all of us know. Josh, get on up here!"

"Me?" I exclaimed, seeing all the faces turn in my direction.

Shan nudged me. "That's what you get for singin' about me and that ol' guitar!"

I jumped up, grinning. "Well, just remember, it was your idea!"

When I joined the musicians and saw everyone's gaze on me, stage fright set in. I looked at Mr. Allsup.

"Uh ... do y'all know 'Kickin' Mule'?"

"Let her rip!" said the mandolin player.

I made it through a couple of verses before I glanced at the lemonade bucket and saw Wally grinning like a silly goose. He was tapping his ear and nodding toward Shan. The rascal! All of a sudden, music was the last thing on my mind. I was thinking sweet nothings and singing sour somethings. I don't think those rafters had ever heard the like of my jumbled squalling. But no matter how loudly I sang, I couldn't drown out Wally's laughter as he pounded out the beat with an exaggerated stomp.

"Gonna poe me some gree-nuts, mighty tall in the

sun," I sang, then realized that wasn't quite right. "Gonna grow me some peanuts"—*There, that's better,* I thought—"mighty tall in the sun. Gonna feed that kickin' mule, and watch it rop and hun—er, hop and run!"

Wally plugged his ears to my strangled-goose yodel, and the song mercifully ended. Everybody clapped—probably because it *had* ended. To a parting pat on my shoulder from Mr. Allsup, I headed back toward Shan. I sat down beside her and saw that cute ear of hers again. Now I was as scared of her as I'd been that day I'd sneaked my first kiss.

"I guess that'll teach you not to stull no more punts—uh, I mean, pull no more stunts," I managed. I had never been so tongue-tied.

She laughed merrily. "Why, we got a mangy ol' cat that sings better than that!"

Again I studied that little ear, half hidden in her blond tresses. "I, uh ... would, uh ... you, uh ..."

"Who's this 'Uh' person you keep talkin' about?" she teased.

"Uh ... uh ..."

She seized my hand and shook it. "Well, nice to meet you, Mr. Uh-uh!"

"Aw, quit your teasin'. Wanna ... wanna take a stroll outside?"

She giggled as we stood and walked out into the cool of the night. The moon had sunk behind the oaks, leaving the crickets chirping in shadows. We stopped at the first big oak and I faced her.

"I-I don't know what's got over me lately, Shan. But I near burned up when that guy got you that punch."

"Why, Josh! You're jealous!"

"Maybe so, but it's all your fault. I can't help it if I love—"

"Don't say that! Don't joke around like that!" Suddenly her voice was awfully serious.

I didn't know what to say. I'd been searching for the courage to whisper in her ear, all right. But the words had slipped out so casually that they had surprised even me.

"We're too young to talk that way!" she went on. "We're too young to be in love when—when I . . . when I've got to—" She grabbed me and held me tightly. "Oh, Josh, don't turn me loose! Please don't ever turn me loose!"

I had never seen such a change come over a person. She was trembling and crying and hanging on as if somebody was trying to yank her away.

"Hey, what's the matter?"

"Oh, Josh, I don't want to leave you, not ever!"

"What are you talkin' about?"

"The bank—they was fixin' to foreclose on Dad! They was takin' the whole farm away from us! He *sold* it, Josh! He called up that cattleman from the Hilldale meetin' and sold out, sold *everything!* Tomorrow, we—we're gonna start movin', all the way to East Texas, my uncle's dairy in Flat Creek!"

"W-what? But he—"

"Just hold me! Hold me and don't ever let go!"

I withdrew just far enough to see her face in the shadows. "No! You can't go off that way! If we was older, we-we'd get mar—"

"Oh, Josh—don't make this any worse than it is!

There's time for all that, a year, two or three years from now! If ... if we still feel the same about each other, there's time!"

We must have said a lot more to each other that night, but I was in such a daze the words didn't register. All I remember is standing on her porch when I took her home. I offered to come back the next day and help them move, but Shan begged me not to. She said she couldn't bear to tell me goodbye again.

Chapter 10

Test of Faith

The next morning, I moped around as if I'd just lost my best friend—which I had. Ma and Pa had been asleep when I'd come home the night before, so they didn't know the news. I found them leaned over their coffee at the breakfast table.

Ma noticed right off that something was wrong. "You're sure lookin' glum this mornin'. Didn't you have a good time last night, darlin'?"

"It's Shan, Ma. She's leavin'. They've sold out."

Ma dropped her spoon. Pa sat bolt upright.

"Leavin'?" he repeated in disbelief. "Al sold out? He told me he'd *never* sell!"

"The bank, Pa. They was takin' their place away."

Pa slammed his fist to the table, spilling coffee. "Dat-blame it!" He burst to his feet. "Dat-blame this drouth!"

"Luke, please!" said Ma.

"I can't help it, Sarah. This drouth's killin' us all and nobody cares!"

———————⚬~⚬⚬⚬~⚬———————

The days rolled on—hot, dry, lonely days. I couldn't sleep. I couldn't eat. I couldn't think about anything but Shan. I knew Pa saw how low I was feeling. But instead of taking me aside first thing and consoling me, he just seemed more and more wrapped up in his own troubles. It hurt me, because suddenly I didn't feel as important in his eyes as those seventy dusty acres.

It wasn't until Shan was way off in East Texas that he finally brought up the matter. Late one evening, I stepped out on the front porch. Pa was sitting against the corner pillar, spitting tobacco juice. A dry wind swept through his sparse gray hair as he motioned with his head.

"Come here a minute, Josh. I want to talk to you."

I sat down beside him and dangled my legs off the porch. He spat a brown stream to the bare earth and studied me.

"You been walkin' around here like you ain't got nothin' to live for."

I looked down at the splattered dirt. "I *don't* have nothin' to live for, Pa."

He breathed sharply. "That's a bunch of tomfoolery. She's just one girl, Josh. They's gonna be more. You can't keep on mopin' about her that way. There's a lot of other things to worry about—our land here, us keepin' it. She's a fine little girl, all right, but you'll get over her."

"No!" I cried, bursting to my feet to see the shock in his

eyes. "I don't want to get over her! All you think about's this farm anymore! I won't ever get over her—not ever!"

I stormed away to the oaks and wouldn't even look back when he called after me.

Every hot, dry day that followed deepened the lines in Pa's face and widened the rift between us. Even around Ma, he seemed to be holding things in more and more. She'd call him for supper and he wouldn't come. We'd find him standing in the peanut field like a scarecrow, staring with that same scarecrow blankness as dust danced around his legs. Not long ago, he'd been the warmest person I'd known. Now he seemed a thousand miles away.

A week after the incident on the porch, I went into town with Pa. He had gotten a heartbreaking pittance for the cattle, but at least he could square up with Sam Morgan now. "When I die," Pa had told Ma, "I don't intend goin' to the cemetery owin' nobody."

As soon as I followed him into Sam's store, I knew something was wrong. The place looked as if a dust devil had hit it. Shelves were empty. Canned goods stood on the floor. Crates blocked the aisles. Flour sacks buried the counter top.

Pa knitted his brow. "You here, Sam?"

An inner door past a jumble of leather items screeched open and I could smell pipe tobacco.

"That you, Luke?" asked Sam, wading through.

"What are you doin', Mr. Morgan?" I asked.

"Takin' inventory. I'm closin' the store."

"*Closin'*?" repeated Pa as if he hadn't heard right. "Since when?"

Sam puffed on his pipe. "Just can't make a livin' at it no

74

more. Gettin' too old, too. Guess I'll drag out the rockin' chair and go live with one of my daughters."

Pa shook his head. "I'm sorry, Sam. All of us should've knowed you can't make no livin' with us tellin' you to put it on the bill all the time."

"Aw, it ain't your fault, Luke. It's the drouth. It's killin' everybody."

"Yeah," said Pa in disgust. "I know."

"Hear about the rainmaker?" Sam let out a little laugh. "Seems that sometime in the night, he packed up our fifty dollars and took his rig and lit out for greener pastures."

Pa took a sharp breath. "We should've *knowed* better. Sarah tried to tell me, and I wouldn't listen."

"Yeah, well, it's hard knowin' right from wrong some-times." He started to puff his pipe again, but stopped at a sudden thought. "Hey, guess who come in here yesterday. That cattleman from Fort Worth."

The furrows in Pa's face deepened. "Wha'd he want?"

"He's closin' some more sales. Jim Dawson's sold out, and so's Oscar."

"Dat-blame it, Sam, we ain't got no chance!" exclaimed Pa. "I gave my cows away, but it'll be a right smart cold day in blazes before I give my farm away, too!"

Sam nodded. "I hope you make it, Luke. Seems like you got more fight in you than most of us."

Pa's voice quietened. "What I got in me ain't somethin' many people would like to have. Sarah says I'm just stub-born and prideful."

"Well, a man's gotta be what he is. Can't be nothin' else."

Before we left town, Pa stopped at the post office and I

checked the box. The first thing I pulled out was a card from Aunt Mildred in Dallas. But it was the crinkled envelope with the flowery script that made my spirits soar and sink, both at the same time.

It was from Shan!

As soon as we started home, while Pa brooded silently and the dust caked his face, I tore open the envelope and read the single page.

Dear Josh,

You don't know how much I miss you and how much I miss home—though I guess this is home now. Oh, Uncle Dave and Aunt Lucy treat us all right and everything, but it's just not the same.

I think about you all the time. All day long, no matter what I'm doing, all I can see is you.

Oh, Josh! I don't know how I can take it! I don't know hardly anybody here—just mostly Dad and my aunt and uncle. It sure gets lonesome.

Uncle Dave's dairy is a few miles southeast of Murchison, right close to Flat Creek. It's pretty country here. The drouth hasn't hit it as hard. It even rained some last night.

Dad says he hopes y'all don't have to sell, too, but ...
I want to see you so bad!

Shan

Just a few hundred miles away, Shan was thinking about me right that moment! I had to see her again! There just had to be a way, and I was going to find it!

Neither Pa nor I said a thing to each other all the way through the home gate. Leaving him to unhitch the mules, I went in the back door and found Ma making dog bread. It was a poor man's cornbread, with water instead of milk.

"Any mail, Josh?"

I suddenly felt so weary. "Shan. She sent me a letter. Oh, Aunt Mildred, too." I held out the postcard.

Ma must have read the despair in my face as she took it. "For somebody who just got a letter from his girl, you sure look down in the dumps. Didn't it cheer you up to hear from her?"

"I guess. But—" I handed the letter to her. "Here, read it."

She scooted out a chair from the table, sat, and parted the envelope with a puff. As she pulled out the page and unfolded it, I looked out the screen door. Memories flooded me—of home and love and the bond that had always seemed so strong between the four of us until now.

When I turned back to Ma, she was slipping the page into the envelope without comment. But her features showed a lot of concern.

"I want to go see her, Ma. I want to go spend the summer there."

She just sat there, staring at the envelope in her hands.

"Ma? I want to go to Flat Creek, to Shan's, at least till school starts up again. Tell me I can go—please tell me I can go."

She turned to me, and I'd never noticed her age lines so deep before. "You ain't but fifteen, Josh. You know you don't have no business bein' out on your own."

"Grandpa wasn't but thirteen when he left home. He

told me so himself. Anyway, I wouldn't *be* on my own. Mr. Burke's there, and he's Pa's best friend. He'd look out after me, help find me a place to stay. I'll get me a job, maybe right there at her uncle's dairy. I'll send money home and everything. Can I go? Please?"

Her voice became very solemn. "Are you sure you want to? You said anything to your Pa about it yet?"

"I don't know how to. It ... it's like I can't talk to him anymore."

"Yes, I know," said Ma, lowering her gaze for a moment and nodding. "Let me try to talk to him about it, see what he thinks. You know how much he always wanted you to stay and work this farm with him, like he did with Grandpa."

"But I'll be back, and things will be like they always used to be with Pa and me."

Will they? I asked myself. *Will they ever?*

Ma went right on out and discussed it with Pa. But even though he and I were around each other the rest of the day, he wouldn't bring it up. All he seemed to do was cast piercing eyes on me. Every time he did, I just lowered mine and couldn't find the right words.

The subject went ignored on through the fading light of dusk, which brought the nightly song of crickets and our weekly worship service. As always, we gathered around the family Bible on the living room table. Pa thumbed through the rustling pages and stopped with his finger on a passage.

He lifted his eyes to me. "You know the story of Job, Josh?" he asked quietly.

"Part of it." My voice was wearier than ever.

"Tell us what you know about it."

I stared down at the table and rubbed its rough edge. "I know he had everything in the world, and then one day he lost it."

Pa turned to Ma. "How come him to lose everything?"

"It was a test of his faith," she answered.

I looked up and found Pa studying me. "What was the big question Job worried with durin' all his troubles?" he asked.

I shook my head. I just didn't feel like talking.

Pa glanced at the passage. "He wanted to know how come the just and righteous have to suffer. Wha'd he find out?"

I swallowed hard. "Maybe ... maybe God just forsakes them sometimes."

Ma turned to me with furrowed brow. "Sometimes there just ain't no real reason, Josh. There's a lot of evil in this ol' world. Sometimes it just seems to overshadow all the good there is."

Pa rasped his thumb along the Bible. "Y'all think that evil's gonna win out over good?"

Everybody went silent. Even Susie stopped her squirming. I guess we were all dwelling mighty seriously on the matter. Finally Ma straightened and answered.

"It might seem that way sometimes, but sooner or later good's gonna win. Maybe not in this world, but in the next. We got His promise on that."

Pa nodded. "Did Job pass the test of faith?"

"Soon as he finally admitted his self-righteousness," said Ma, "he had everything give back to him, and more, 'cause of the Lord's love."

"That's right," said Pa, studying us solemnly. "And we oughta not ever forget that, no matter what."

He closed the Bible and slid it to the center of the table. "Now," he said, folding his arms in front of it, "y'all have any problems you want to talk about?"

It was the same question Pa asked at nearly every family worship, but this time it seemed directed just at me. I had a *big* matter to discuss, and half a dozen times in that long silence I started to speak. But when I didn't, Ma did.

"Well, *I* got somethin' to talk about." She pulled a postcard out of her dress pocket and laid it next to the Bible. "Mildred wrote. I told her how tough things are. She said Alma told her there was a new factory in Dallas hirin'. She said you might get a job with it, Luke, and that, anyway, we could go live with them till things get straightened out."

"No!" snapped Pa, slamming his fist on the table and jumping up. "We ain't gonna leave!"

Ma seemed stunned by his outburst. "I know I ain't ever talked like this before. I know that, Luke. I don't want to leave, neither, but there just ain't no way here no more—no way at all."

"I ain't gonna scrounge off of 'em, Sarah—I just won't! I'll die first!"

"And Susie," said Ma, running her fingers through Sue-Sue's golden curls, "you gonna let her die, too?"

Pa exhaled sharply and turned away.

"What's *happened* to this family?" asked Ma, looking

first at Pa and then at me. "Why is it we can't talk about things no more? Family worship's supposed to bring us together, but it's got so we can't even *talk* about our problems with each other!"

I looked at the sadness in her eyes, and then at Pa as he stood with his back to us. Then my words came, hoarse and blunt.

"Can't you see we're dyin' here, Pa?"

He turned, and I had to make myself face him.

"Things didn't used to be this way!" I cried. "We used to be happy, even if we didn't have nothin'! The drouth's killin' us, Pa. It's killin' us all."

He just stood there, silent and staring. Finally he passed his hand over his face and looked at Ma.

"Okay, Sarah," he said quietly. "You take the kids and go stay with Mildred till this drouth's over."

"You know I won't do that, Luke! No matter what, a wife's place is with her husband!"

"Even when the Lord's forsaken him?" he snapped bitterly.

It was time to tell him, I knew. I took a deep breath and looked down. My fingers trembled against the table.

"I . . . I want to go away, Pa. I want to go where Shan's at."

I could almost feel his eyes piercing me. "That what you want to do?" he asked bitterly.

I nodded without finding his gaze.

"Okay," he said curtly. "I'll do everything I can to help you out, Josh."

I was leaving! I was really leaving!

Chapter 11

Pretty Little Thing

Two days later, I stood before a passenger train at the red-brick depot in nearby Comanche. From up-track, I could hear steam hissing and the bang of railcars coupling up. I had a battered old suitcase in my hand and a lot of butterflies in my stomach. But I put on my best face for my folks, who had come to see me off.

Ma had all but insisted I write the Burkes first, but I talked her out of it. Every day I waited was another day away from Shan. But Pa had put his foot down when I'd said I wanted to hitchhike to Flat Creek, a couple of hundred miles east. "If you're goin' out in the world," he'd told me, "don't do it like a hobo." He had proceeded to trade a couple of chickens to the depot agent for a ticket.

The porter brushed by on his way to a nearby passenger car. "Better hurry, folks."

I lowered the suitcase and picked up Susie and her little doll with the button eyes. "You be good, Sue-Sue. You stay out of those sandstorms, you hear?"

"I be good, Joss."

I tickled her feet, then set her down and turned to Ma. "Well, guess I better get on."

I met her halfway and we hugged. I could feel the moisture at her eyes as she brushed against my cheek. "You look real nice in them Sunday clothes," she said, her voice breaking. "We're gonna miss you, Josh."

"Aw, Ma."

The train whistle pierced the morning.

"There's the whistle," said Pa. "Better get on." He put out his hand. I took it, then melted into his arms and he hugged me. For a moment, he didn't seem to want to let go.

The whistle blew again. I picked up the suitcase and climbed aboard. I stood on the steps and looked back, realizing I had forgotten to tell them I loved them. Then the train lurched forward and they called out "bye." Suddenly I was so choked up that all I could do was lift a hand in a halfhearted wave. They receded down the track, then the porter touched my arm and I went on into the passenger car.

All the way through Dallas and on into Murchison, a line from a Jimmie Rodgers song played in my mind:

For I'm lonesome and blue for some place to roam,
And I wish it could be down the old road to home.

And here I was, traveling the road *away* from home as fast as a barreling locomotive. I could only pray I was doing right.

It was a funny feeling stepping off the train a stranger in Murchison. But I was sure getting excited about seeing Shan. I asked directions to Flat Creek at the depot and soon was walking a sandy lane through gums and pines and past green fields of cotton. It felt good to be in a country so alive. All the way through timbered stretches, I could hear the rustle of birds flitting through dogwood shrubs. In swampy hollows, where river birches crawled with mustang grapevines, I could even taste dampness in the air.

For a long time, only the afternoon sun and the buzz of cicadas went with me. Then, as a scissortail dived to fuss at a bullsnake just off the road, I heard the clatter of a vehicle behind me. I turned at the screeching of brakes. A battered old truck stopped alongside, framing the driver through the open passenger's window.

"Want a ride?"

The driver was a cheerful-looking fellow in his mid-sixties with sparse gray hair and large ears. There were a lot of laugh lines in his stubbly face.

"Yes, sir, sure do."

I tossed my suitcase in the bed and hopped in. He shifted into gear and the truck lurched down the road.

"Just come from town?" he drawled.

"Yes, sir. Got off a passenger train there."

"Just been over to Murchison myself. Drive over from Flat Creek ever' day and deliver my milk." He glanced at a cow ambling down the borrow ditch. "You visitin' in these parts?"

"Yes, sir, up from Comanche County."

He looked surprised. "Oh? You wouldn't happen to know a family by the name of Burke, would you?"

I'd never been so surprised. "Why, I sure do!"

"Well, Al's my youngest brother."

Of all people to be hitching a ride with, I was in the same truck as Shan's uncle Dave!

I held out my right hand. "You're Mr. Dave Burke, aren't you?"

He took my hand in his calloused palm and looked puzzled. "Why, yes—sure am. How'd—"

"Josh Watson. They had the next farm over from us. I come down to see Shan."

He grinned, showing a missing front tooth. "Well, I swan! I've heard Al speak of your pa lots of times! He sure thinks a lot of him."

"Me, too," I said. Suddenly I felt so guilty I wanted to crawl away and hide.

"So! You come over to see Shan, have you?"

"Yes, sir, and to get some work for the summer, I hope."

"She's a pretty little thing, isn't she? Reckon she's got fellers chasin' after her all over the country."

He must have caught the jealous look in my face. "Whoops!" he added. "I say something wrong?"

"She ... she's sure pretty, all right," I managed to say.

He grinned again and looked down the road. "Yep, seems like ever' time Al and her come to see us, all the boys would try to corral her. Already been a couple over since they moved down."

I cringed. She was *my* girl!

"Say, son," he said, breaking my thoughts, "where you stayin' while you're here?"

The question came so casually that I know I looked

confused. I'd intended to stay at least a while with the Burkes—all of them. But I'd just read in his words that it had never crossed his mind. I realized now how nervy it had been of me to expect a total stranger to give me a place to sleep. Pa wouldn't have imposed that way!

I guess I went silent for a long time, because the old gent spoke up again. "Son?"

"Oh, uh," I groped for an answer, "I'm ... supposed to ... uh ... go to work for a man not far from Flat Creek." Pa had taught me never to lie. I wondered if he would have understood.

"Oh, is that right? That wouldn't be ol' man Jackson, would it? I hear he's been lookin' for somebody to help out around his farm there."

"Uh ... yes, sir, I ... uh ... *think* ... that's his name." Feeling shame for telling another lie, I dropped my gaze and wondered for the first time if I wouldn't have been better off staying at home.

"Well, the Jackson place is a couple of miles this side of mine. Reckon you want me to let you off there for now, don't you?"

"Uh ... well, I ... uh ... kind of wanted to see Shan today."

"Well, she's was leavin' to go horseback ridin' with one of the neighbor boys when I left. Said she wouldn't be back till dark. Reckon you'll have to wait till tomorrow."

I started as if a cattle prod had caught me in the ribs. What had he said? Shan riding with a boy?

For a long time, I just stared blankly out the side window, my self-doubt building. We passed the close-set frame houses of Flat Creek community and dipped through the low-water crossing of a tangled hollow. On a flat stretch of tilled land beyond, I caught the glare of the sun from a tin-roofed farmhouse.

"There's the Jackson place," he said. "See that new barn he's put up?"

Right that moment I started to tell him the truth. But how could I brand myself a liar in the eyes of Shan's uncle? Pa had been right. Even a little lie can be like a snowball, getting bigger the farther a person lets it go.

The brakes screeched and the elder Burke pulled up beside a bent mailbox on the right. Through the rotting slats of a picket fence wound with ivy, I saw an L-shaped house with high gables and a screened-in porch. The whole place looked as if it had never seen paint.

"Well, son," he said, smiling pleasantly, "good luck on your new job. I'll tell Al and Shan I seen you today."

"Uh ..." My hand was on the door, but I couldn't bring myself to push it open. "I ... uh ..." Again I started to tell him the truth. But once more the fear of being caught in a lie kept me from it. "Thank ... thanks for the ride, Mr. Burke."

I opened the door and got out. I stood there in the exhaust fumes, and the truck pulled away. I watched the sand fly from its tires until it reeled around a bend a quarter-mile away.

With a wag of my head, I faced the house and didn't know what to do. I reached for the gate latch and my hand shook. The gate creaked inward on rusty hinges, and I took a deep breath and started for the screened-in porch.

All of a sudden I heard the threatening bark of a dog. The next thing I knew, a snarling black mutt with powerful jaws burst around the corner of the house. Before I could whirl to run, I was facing a vicious animal that wanted to take my leg off.

"Get away!" I cried.

Its flashing teeth went for my leg and ripped open my Sunday pants. I fended it off with my suitcase and yelled again. Then the screen door popped and I heard the shout of a gruff voice.

"Roscoe! Roscoe! Gol-durn it! Git over here!"

A gray-haired man with a crooked jaw and a face as mean as the dog's stood on the steps. The dog cowered at his words and slowly slunk toward him with its tail tucked between its legs. When it reached the steps, the man seized it by the collar and glared at me.

"If it's a handout you're lookin' for, you can just get on out of here," he snapped, in the same tone he'd used with the dog.

"I . . . uh . . . I was lookin' for a . . . for a job."

The dog squirmed, and he readjusted his grip on the collar. "You ain't gonna find it *here*. When I hire somebody it's gonna be a *man*." With that, he turned and dragged the dog through the door.

It had all been so quick that I just stood there for a minute, stunned. Then, through the screen of the porch, I heard the growl of the dog again and I hurried for the lane.

I felt so lost and afraid. I glanced at the sun, sinking into a heavy cloud in the west. Soon it would be dark. Where was I going to stay? What was I going to I eat?

Shaken, I began walking the lane to the south again, tracing the tread marks of Dave Burke's truck. Before I'd gone half a mile, the suitcase grew so heavy I edged off the road and sat down in a tangled thicket. I was miserable. I leaned back wearily against a sweet gum and stared at the almost-hidden road through dogwood leaves and thorny underbrush. I could smell rotting vegetation and feel the damp, mildewed leaves of years past through what was left of my Sunday britches.

Just as my empty stomach growled, I heard hoofbeats and faint voices back up the road. In moments, a big bay gelding came into view.

When I saw the bouncing ponytail of its rider, my heart went to pounding like Wally Fingers' boot stomping out "Kickin' Mule." It was Shan!

My first instinct was to call out and run into the road. Then I saw the barrel-chested teenager on the roan behind her and I stayed hidden. He was really eyeing her, and my blood started to boil. With that thin red mustache, buck teeth, and sloping chin, he was sure nothing to look at.

"So, does this mean we're going together now?" he asked as they came abreast of me. His nasal voice was so annoying!

"Whoa!" exclaimed Shan. "Who said anything about me bein' sweet on you, Danny?"

"Aw, come on," he insisted as they passed. "You like me and you know it."

I wanted to drag him off that horse!

Her saddle creaked as she turned. She gave him the same smile she'd given me a hundred times. "Of course I like you!"

Stunned, I just sat there and watched them ride away. *Shan!* I cried silently. *Shan!*

I lay back in the rotting leaves and folded my forearm across my eyes. I was confused and angry and hurt. Shan with somebody else! I was so lost in emotion that I didn't even know when the sun sank and dark crept across the land. I kept replaying that troubling scene in my mind, finding it harder to accept every time. I guess I finally lapsed into fitful sleep.

The next thing I knew, thunder was blaring and rain was pelting me in the face. I bolted up in a rushing wind. It was pitch black, but all around I could hear the thrashing of brush and groaning of limbs. Lightning cracked, and I could see rain sweeping across the road in sheets. Then everything went dark again and thunder shook the ground.

I dragged the suitcase in close to the sweet gum bole. All I could do was hunker there, flinching every time lightning cracked. What a cruel joke this was. Rain had forsaken our farm. It had torn my family apart and driven me here. Now it came in a torrent, only to catch me unprotected so far from where it could have done any good.

Suddenly I came to my senses. What was I doing here? I'd come all this way to see Shan, not to squat under some tree and let the rain drench me. So *what* if she liked that fellow? She had a mangy old cat she liked, too!

I grabbed my suitcase and broke through the whipping limbs. The sandy lane was like a river, but it would lead me to the Burke place. As I started down it, I cringed to a sharp sting at my collarbone. All of a sudden, pea-sized hail was pounding down out of a black sky. It fell in a fury, hard rocks that bounced off my shoulders and skull. I threw my suitcase over my head and pressed on, wincing every time a stone caught my exposed fingers.

Buffeted by the wind, I sloshed along the flowing lane for several minutes before it carried me down into a hollow. Here, overhanging branches hid even the popping lightning, forcing me to feel my way through the dark. But I could hear more than ever. The hail, the wind, the driving rain—everything seemed to clamor louder with every step. It was almost like a freight train was in front of me.

At first the submerged road had run ankle-deep. But now the water had climbed to my shins and developed an odd crossways surge. I went on a few more steps toward that thundering train and felt the rising flow pushing harder and harder against me. All of a sudden it was up to my thighs and too strong, and I went off balance with a cry.

I hung on to my suitcase with one hand and went under. I came up coughing and the water swept me into clawing briars and pummeling brush. I yelled, but my cry died in a tumult more violent than any freight train. *A flash flood, Pa! Pa, a flash flood's got me!*

It was roaring across the road and carrying me with it. I was bobbing and gasping and catching limbs in my face, and I was helpless to do anything but flail wildly in the dark.

I was going to drown!

Chapter 12

Quite a Girl

I went under and stayed. Dark water swirled all around. But I could see Pa and Ma and Susie clearly. They were back home dying of drouth while I was dying in more water than I'd ever seen. I could hear the muffled bedlam around me and taste the bitter mud all the way into my stomach.

Suddenly the buoyant suitcase caught hard on something above. It slipped, and slipped again, then lodged firm. The force almost ripped my arm from my shoulder, but somehow I held on. The next thing I knew, I was bobbing in place with a mountain of water rushing in my face. I was gasping air and swallowing mud almost in the same breath. My legs were straight out behind me, thrashing in the violent flow.

I lunged in the dark for whatever it was that gripped my suitcase. I found a knotty limb and seized it. Bouncing at water level, it seemed to stretch at a right angle across the current. I traded my suitcase for a two-handed grasp and pulled myself to the bough. It was thicker on the left, leading me to fight my way toward its strength. After a harried minute, I reached the bole and dragged myself out of the raging flood.

I'd made it!

I lay there for long seconds, shivering and coughing and spitting out mud. The hail had eased, but a hard rain still fell from the rumbling sky. I was worried about my lost suitcase as I started on for the Burkes'. But I sure wouldn't have traded places with it.

I sloshed down that dark, stormy road for terrible minutes. Finally the lane made a bend to the east and a flash of lightning showed outlines ahead. There was a modest rock house and large barn along a right-side ridge overlooking a shallow valley. I came to a mailbox with the name Burke and waded through a muddy yard to a covered porch. I started to knock, but the windows were all dark. Storm or no storm, I wasn't going to compound my misdeeds by waking everybody up.

I went back out into the rain and followed a little road running with water to the barn. A stream poured from its roof to drench old tractor parts. I could hear loose tin clattering in the howling wind. Everything was in shadow, but with the help of lightning, I found a side door and went in.

It was even darker inside. I clapped my hands to wake any rattlesnakes, then groped over to a stall. Curling up in loose hay, I drifted off to sleep to the pounding of rain on the roof.

I was a muddy mess as morning broke bright and I knocked on the Burkes' door. In a few seconds it creaked inward, and I was suddenly face-to-face with Shan. That sweet smile and dangling ponytail were a mighty welcome sight after all I'd been through since nightfall.

"Josh!" she cried excitedly, rushing out. Then she saw my ripped pants and all the caked mud. "What on earth you been into? You look like somethin' the cats drug in!"

I glanced down at my clothes and shrugged. "So much for my Sunday best."

"I wasn't able to sleep all night—ever since Uncle Dave told me you was here!"

"I didn't sleep much, either," I said with a grin. Only now could I find a little humor in my troubles.

"I still can't believe you're here! How long can you stay?"

"Till school starts, anyway. Everything sure seemed to fall apart when y'all moved away. Now we can pick up where we left off."

She developed an odd little frown that I'd never seen on her before. She went silent and lowered her gaze.

"Gosh," I added, "you don't know how I much I missed you. I sure liked your letter."

She looked up. "How ... how's your folks doin'?" Her voice was quiet all of a sudden.

"Not too good. Pa's afraid he's fixin' to lose our place, too."

We made small-talk for three or four minutes, but

something seemed to be missing. Her initial excitement had faded. The spark was gone from her voice, and the sparkle from her eyes. All spring, we'd been like a well-oiled machine. Now all we seemed to do was sputter and clatter.

"You seem kind of . . . I don't know, quiet or somethin' this mornin'," I finally said. "What's the matter?"

Again came that little frown, this time with a sigh and another glance down. "How . . . how come you didn't write me first?"

"I . . . uh . . ." Now I felt pretty insecure. "I guess I was in too big a hurry to get here."

That pretty chin of hers started to quiver. "The least you could've done was *ask*, Josh."

"I . . . I guess I *am* puttin' your uncle out quite a bit."

"I don't mean that. I mean askin' about . . . you and me."

Now it was my turn to frown. "What about us?"

Suddenly she wouldn't look at me. "You . . . you shouldn't've come all this way like that. Not if you expect . . . " She turned away. "Things, they just change all of a sudden sometimes, Josh. Don't you know that?"

"What are you talkin' about?"

She wouldn't answer, but I was afraid I already knew. That scene in the road was playing in my mind.

"So is it *him*?" I asked.

Only now did she look up, and I could tell she was puzzled.

In an instant, all the hurt and anger I'd felt beside the lane came over me. "I was there by the road," I snapped, "wore out after ridin' a train all day to come see you. Y'all came ridin' by, and I saw and heard plenty."

Now her chin trembled even worse, and she turned away with hanging head.

"Well, I'll be dogged, Josh!"

I turned to the swinging screen door and found Al Burke framed in the threshold. I tried to speak, but my voice wouldn't work.

"How's Luke makin' it?" he asked.

My spirits sank deeper, but at least I could talk now. "Things are gettin' rougher."

He nodded sadly. "Life sure ain't a easy thing, is it? Sure wish we could've both found us a job somewhere."

He invited me in for breakfast. I'd lost my appetite and maybe a whole lot more, but I was also weak from going without food. Leaving Shan alone on the porch, I went on in. When she followed a few minutes later, her eyes were red and her cheeks were blotched.

Dave Burke and his wife showed me a lot of hospitality. They let me clean up and loaned me some clothes. But I also noticed how sparse the breakfast table was. This was the Great Depression, and times were hard everywhere.

I don't think I looked up at Shan during the whole meal. Mostly I talked to her dad about Pa and the drouth, and to her uncle about Jackson turning me away.

"Tell you what, son," said the elder Burke. "I'll run you up to Jackson's place after a while and make sure the ol' geezer hires you."

When he and I left in his old truck later that morning, I looked back. Shan stood on the porch, watching us drive away. Her usual smile was gone, and only hurt and confusion were in its place. We hadn't spoken again, and I felt just terrible about it all.

The creek in the hollow where I'd almost drowned was still running a little high, but we managed to ford it. Soon Shan's uncle pulled the sputtering truck to a stop next to the bent mailbox at the Jackson place.

"Wait here while I go talk to him," he said, getting out. "He's a cantankerous ol' coot sometimes. But I'll get you that job, one way or another."

I turned to scout the yard. "He's got a dog that'll take your leg off, Mr. Burke," I warned.

He reached in the cab as if he already knew and honked the horn. Sure enough, the black mutt came running, barking viciously. But at least the commotion roused the farmer. The porch door opened and Jackson stepped outside, his face as mean as ever. He called the dog and seized it by the collar, allowing Mr. Burke to go in the gate.

The two men met in the yard. They talked, or maybe they argued. Jackson slung his arm in my direction a couple of times. The thick veins in his neck seemed ready to burst. But I guess Shan's uncle was the more stubborn, because Jackson finally nodded. A moment later, Mr. Burke was on his way back to the truck. When he reached it, he stuck his head in the window.

"Well, son, he's gonna try you out for a week or so. That's the best I could do."

"Thanks, Mr. Burke. Thanks a lot."

"Don't forget your tow sack with your clothes and all in it."

"Yes, sir. I sure appreciate it."

A couple of minutes later, I was alone in the yard with a britches-eating dog and a farmer who looked ready to bite my head off. Right then I was more worried about the snarling dog.

Jackson nodded to the animal. "Let him sniff you. Go on! Do like I say and he'll settle down!"

I wasn't so sure, but I edged closer and the dog's wet nose smeared a trail along my leg.

"I-I'm Josh Watson."

"I'm Mister Jackson to you. I'll treat you fair if you treat me the same."

"Yes, sir."

"Pay's fifty cents a day plus eats and a place to sleep. Any complaints?"

"No, sir."

"Okay, then. You'll find a little store room back of the house with a cot in it. Go ahead and put your stuff in it so's we can get to work."

Fifty cents a day! At that rate, I'd have enough to buy a place of my own in about fifty years. But I knew there were a lot of people in the nation who would have given their eye teeth for a job that paid any amount. And Pa was one of them.

I don't think I'd ever worked so hard in my life as I did that day. I shoveled manure, carried rocks, and dug post holes till the sweat poured. I'd done the same kind of work before, but not with somebody breathing down my neck. He was ready to yell at me if I made a single mis-lick. I was so tired by evening that I almost went to sleep milking his old Jersey. I found his wife kinder and gentler, though. She insisted I take extra helpings at the supper table.

All through that long, muggy day, I thought about Shan. I knew I hadn't handled the situation very well. Maybe I'd gotten the wrong idea about things. I'd accused her and she hadn't gotten a chance to explain. We were best friends, and friends didn't snap at each other the way I'd done with her. I knew I'd never be able to sleep again till we thrashed things out. I'd start by telling her I was sorry.

By the time supper ended, it was dusk. I was so tired I could hardly stand, but I cleaned up anyway and started walking to the Burkes'. The hoot of an owl and the brightening stars went with me. Hard dark found me at their porch. The wood door was open, and I could see a flickering lamp inside. I silently rehearsed my apology and knocked.

Al Burke appeared at the door. "Well, evenin', Josh! Come on in!"

"That's okay. I just came by to see Shan. She around?"

He frowned and groped for words. "I . . . uh . . . She's out by the barn, I think. Why don't you come in and wait for her?"

"No, thanks. I'm real tired. I'll just go on out there."

I started away, but Mr. Burke followed after me. "Why don't you come on in for a little bit? We got a pot of coffee perkin'."

I faced him again. "I appreciate it, Mr. Burke, but I just need to talk to Shan a minute."

He took a deep breath and came closer, his face solemn in the lamplight. "You can't go out there, Josh."

I frowned.

"I know what you think of her and all," he went on, "and I don't blame you a bit, 'cause she's quite a girl, all right. But there's ... uh ... others that might think that, too."

I stared at him for the brief seconds it took for his words to sink in. When they did, it nearly killed me. I backed away, a hand at my brow, then everything went to whirring and I clutched a pillar to steady myself.

"I know it's hard on you, Josh, but she don't mean to hurt you. She's young—so are you. You both got your whole lives ahead of you."

I didn't say another word. I just reeled away with lowered head and found the steps. When I reached the lane, the door spring creaked and I knew he had gone back inside.

Meanwhile, I had been dwelling on things. The more I brooded, the angrier I got. Suddenly I directed it all at a barrel-chested fellow I didn't even know. Whirling, I ran for the barn.

I'd fought for Shan once, and I wouldn't give up so easy!

Chapter 13

All the Wrong Reasons

The glow of the moon had never seemed this harsh.

It rose through shrubby oaks, a flattened ball of orange that burned like a drouthy sun. Framed against it, on a big, flat rock at the rim of a gully, were a girl and a boy. They snuggled so close that I could hardly tell them apart.

I stepped out from the corner of the barn and found courage I didn't know I had.

"Hi," I rasped.

Both of them started and whirled.

"Josh!" Shan exclaimed, jumping to her feet. "You scared me!"

I sank inside as I studied her friend. "I ... I don't think we've met."

Even in the moonlight, I could see her jaw drop. She cast a quick glance at him and her chin began to quiver. Then she lowered her gaze and her voice was just a whisper. "This . . . this is . . ." The words hung in her throat, and she turned away.

I could tell the broad-chested guy was puzzled, because he looked at her strangely. But he stepped forward with an outstretched hand. "Danny Lester. Who are you?"

I ignored him and looked over his shoulder at Shan. "I . . . I guess I didn't get things wrong, after all."

"Oh, Josh!" she sobbed without turning. "You don't understand! You just don't understand!"

"What else is there?" I gave the boy a piercing stare.

He took a step closer, standing over me menacingly. He was a head taller and a lot broader in the shoulders. "You trying to start something? Who the thunder you think you are?"

"Ask her."

He crowded me even more. "I don't know what your trouble is, but take it somewhere else!"

All of a sudden, he shoved me hard in the chest.

I staggered back, then lowered my shoulder and charged him like a fullback hitting the line. It was a knee-jerk reaction, but that still didn't make it right. I rammed him hard in the stomach and knocked the breath out of him with a loud *humpf!* My momentum drove him right off that bluff. I turned loose and caught myself on my hands and knees as he fell back. I could hear him tumbling head over heels through shrubs and rocks all the way down.

"Danny!" cried Shan, spinning just in time to see me drive him over the rim. She found my eyes in the moonlight. "How could you, Josh! I never want to see you again! Not ever!"

She scrambled away down the bluff. Then there was nothing I could do anymore but get up and walk away.

Well, there was *one* thing I could do. I could add disappointment in myself to all the burdens I already carried.

———⚬⚬⚬⚬⚬———

I tossed and turned on that hard cot all night, worrying what to do. Did I tuck my tail between my legs and go home, when I had a paying job? If I stayed and toughed it out, I could send Pa a little money each week. It wouldn't pull him out of his fix, but it would help.

But something else was at play in my mind. I just couldn't go back this quick and tell Pa I'd been wrong. I guess I was too proud for my own good. Maybe it was all a matter of being my father's son.

So I stayed, working from sunup to sunset seven days a week. The only time I ever set foot off the place was the one day I went into Murchison with Jackson to pick up supplies.

I bought an envelope and stamp from Mrs. Jackson late one evening and wrote home. I didn't mention Shan. I just sent them my wages and included the route number of Jackson's mailbox out of Murchison.

I was chopping weeds behind the barn a week later when Jackson came up with two letters. One was from Ma; the other had no return address. Out of curiosity, I opened the latter first. It read:

Dear Josh:
I know you don't want to see me, so that's why I'm

*writing. I'm sorry about the other night. Thank goodness
y'all are okay. But I guess there's lots of ways to get hurt.
The last thing I ever want to do is hurt you. You've always
meant so much to me!*

*Please don't be mad at me. I just couldn't go through
life knowing you were mad at me. I'll always be your
friend, and I hope I can still call you my best friend. Life's
too short to lose people you care about!*

God bless you, Josh. I know He's looking out for us both.

I stared at Shan's signature until it became a blur. I'd
already started a letter to her. Now I'd finish it and apolo-
gize and tell her that she was still *my* best friend, too. I'd
had a lot of time to cool off since that night at the barn.

I had also borrowed Mrs. Jackson's Bible one evening
and read over Ma's favorite verse, Romans 8:28: "We know
that all things work together for good to them that love
God." It had sure helped me feel better about things. Now
Shan's letter reinforced what I already knew—the Good
Lord, and nobody else, was in control. All I had to do was
trust Him, and He'd see me through all these lingering
feelings of rejection.

But, as Ma always said, God works in mysterious ways.
Little did I know that Ma's letter would hint at something
that would change the course of my life yet again.

*... Don't know what's wrong with the windmill, but
it's about quit pumping. Your pa's going to pull it once
he gets some new leathers. Sure wish you was here to*

help him, Josh. He's getting too old to climb around on that thing like he used to.

Three days later, I was between the elevated tank and the barn, digging a trench for a water line. The sun was a ball of fire through the whirring windmill. I'd just leaned against my shovel to wipe my sweaty forehead when a dark Ford pulled up in front of the house. A man in khakis got out and started for the gate, only to spot me and veer in my direction. It was good to see somebody different for a change.

"Howdy!" I called out as he neared. Only then did the glint of sunlight call my attention to his badge and sidearm. By the time he stopped in front of me, I could read the "Sheriff's Department" patch at his shoulder.

"Morning," he said. He glanced at a fluttering paper in his hand. "Got a emergency message for Josh Watson."

I never knew the summer sun could turn so cold. "I . . . I'm Josh."

I read strange regret in his hawk-like face. He handed me the paper and nodded to the road. "I'll be over in the car for a couple of minutes if there's anything I can do, son."

I was alone with the crinkled page. I let the shovel drop and sank to the mound of loose dirt alongside the trench. With terrible fear, I turned the page with trembling fingers and found the typed words.

Josh:
   Your pa fell from windmill. Hurt bad. Come quick.

                                                    Ma

"Pa!" My chest was so tight I could hardly breathe. "Oh, Pa!"

I buried my face against that rustling page and whispered his name until the word just wouldn't come any more.

All the way back to Comanche on a passenger train, I stared through the window and heard that same song in my mind:

> *For I'm lonesome and blue for some place to roam,*
> *And I wish it could be down the old road to home.*

Home! Finally that's just where I was headed. But I was going back for all the wrong reasons. It had taken a taste of life on my own and an awful tragedy to make me realize just how sweet home really was.

The sun was hanging low over our wind-swept fields when a truck driver dropped me off at the front gate. It could have been the same cattle truck that had hauled Sal away. I never asked, because I wasn't sure I really wanted to know.

A couple of minutes later, I was at the front door. I went in without fanfare and found Ma sitting at the kitchen table, her back half-turned.

"I'm home, Ma."

She spun with all sorts of emotion in her puffy eyes and drawn face. "Josh!" she cried, jumping up.

I met her halfway. I'd never dreamed that her arms tight around me could have felt so good.

"Oh, darlin'! You don't have no idea how much I've missed you!"

"How's Pa?"

She shook her head. "He ain't doin' good at all. Doctor's been out twice today. He's got a broke leg, a separated shoulder, some cracked ribs, I think. He'd been bleedin' inside, too, but that's startin' to cure up a little."

"I ... I need to talk to him."

Her eyes began to glisten. "He's been needin' to talk to you too, darlin'. He's in the back room."

When I went in the little corner bedroom with blue wallpaper and yellow curtains, it was as if I'd just walked up to the foot of Pa's grave. His heels and upturned toes faced me. He stretched out and away on a four-post bed that took up almost the entire room. His arm was in a sling, and a splint covered his leg.

"Pa? I ... I'm here."

He raised his head weakly and a smile crossed his puffed lips. "Josh," he said, slowly lifting an arm to me. "Come here. I knowed you'd be comin'."

I went to his bedside and winced when I saw all the bruising around his eyes. He extended a trembling hand. It wasn't enough for me. I hugged him, wishing I could do so many things over again.

"I ... I left you, Pa. You needed me and I left you."

He took a deep breath and grimaced to the pain. "Aw, don't do yourself thataway," he said slowly, as if it hurt to talk. "Ain't your fault. Anyhow, doctor tells me a few weeks of takin' it easy and I'll be up and about. Meantime, you gotta look out after your ma and Susie."

I glanced down and the guilt came again. "How ... how you feelin'?"

"Aw, just ain't no punk right now." But he forced a smile. "Feelin' better now that you're here, though."

"Ma said you fell?"

"Slipped, just plumb slipped. I was gonna put some windmill oil in, and there I went. Just gettin' too old to climb around on them things."

I hung my head, for that's exactly what Ma had told me in her letter.

"How's Al gettin' along?" he asked. "Shan?"

I looked up. "We ... we broke up, Pa. Just like that."

Suddenly there was a lot of concern in his face. "Doggone it." He shook his head and sighed. "I know it bothers you, Josh. I'm sure sorry." Then he looked straight into my eyes. "I'm sorry about a *lot* of things. I should-n't've been so wrapped up in my troubles to where I wasn't doin' you and your ma and Susie right."

"No, Pa, it was *my* doin'. I was wrong. I shouldn't ought to have ever left. We're gonna keep this place. We ain't gonna *ever* sell it. I'll work this place right alongside you like you done with Grandpa."

I was surprised to see Pa shake his head. "No, Josh. You was right. You was right all along. We're dyin' here. We're dyin' and we're leavin'."

I flinched. "What—"

"We're packin' up and goin'. Wally was over to see me today. I had him call up that cattleman for me. Sometime this week that fellow's bringin' them papers over for signin'."

I was stunned. "You can't! Y-you just can't!"

"I was wrong, that's all there is to it. You tried to tell me, but I wouldn't listen. I should've knowed all along you can't beat this drouth."

"But we can! You and me together! I won't ever run out on you no more!"

He shook his head yet again. "We tried ever' way in the world, you know that. That lawmaker was supposed to march in and see the governor soon as he got re-elected. Doomsday could come and we'd still be waitin' on him. You told me we was dyin' here, and it took a fall from the windmill to make me see it."

"But I was wrong!"

He forced a smile and reached for my hand. "I'm at peace about it, Josh. Your ma and me prayed together, and I'm at peace about it."

I looked away, shaken. All kinds of crazy ideas ran through my mind.

Pa's tired sigh brought me turning. "I'm afraid I'm about to go to sleep on you, son. Doctor give me some kind of pill."

I looked into his gray eyes. "I'm sorry about everything, Pa—real sorry."

In answer, he squeezed my hand and smiled.

I went to the door. As I opened it with a creak, he quietly called my name. I turned to his swollen face.

"I'm glad you're home, Josh," he said. "Real glad."

My jaw began to tremble, and the words came only in a whisper. "Me, too, Pa."

But I wasn't *staying* home. I knew I had a job to do!

Chapter 14

Trouble Brewing

I could hear the barreling freight train long before I could see it in the night.

I huddled under a dripping water tank beside the track, a lot of moonlit miles from home. I had walked out the door without a word to anyone. Down those southbound rails, a hundred and fifty miles, lay Austin and Governor Ma Ferguson. I had let Pa down once, but I wouldn't this time. Maybe no lawmaker cared enough about our troubles to march in and see the governor, but there was one fifteen-year-old who did care.

Nothing was going to stop me.

I had a few dollars in my pocket, enough for passenger fare. But what I didn't have was time. Freights ran from Comanche to Austin every night, but passenger trains only twice a week. That cattleman would be showing up with those sale papers any day!

I sprang to my feet as the bright headlight burst over a hill a half-mile away. I ran for the shielding brush and found a shadowy tangle of briary oaks. Crouching, I felt the bite of thorns as I watched the approach of that single light in the night and its trailing black wall of railcars.

Soon I could smell the cinders belching from the chugging locomotive. I could see sparks flying from the track and feel the ground shake. I could hear the *clickety-click* of rolling wheels and the piercing screech of a sagging rail.

It was a freight train in all its might—and I was about to steal a ride.

The boxcars were as big as barns. The great iron wheels kept the rails polished to a fine sheen. But the inside flanges that held the wheels firm against the rails could do more than grind. They could cut a man in half, or so Wally Fingers had said. Wally had told me plenty about his hoboing days.

The locomotive groaned to a stop at the water tower. Two figures emerged with a swinging lantern. I watched as they set to work watering the steam engine by means of a large spout that dropped from the overhead tank. While the brakemen were busy, I looked up the line and started to worry. I couldn't see a single open boxcar.

Within minutes, the brakemen were finished. They boarded the locomotive, and the lantern's glow went with them. Once again, the boxcars were just shadows in the moonlight.

I darted out of the brush to the hiss of steam. I tested the nearest boxcar door and gained only splinters. But now I had new respect for the danger of hopping a moving freight. A boxcar rode so far off the ground! Under my rib cage, the car gave way to open space, so close to those iron wheels. If I tried to mount a chest-high platform, my legs were sure to swing underneath. Those wheels were ready to butcher!

I ran on up the line, finding only locked doors. Suddenly, with a jolt that banged couplings tight, the box-cars lurched forward. The rails creaked as the wheels began to track along. I stopped and watched the cars roll by, picking up speed. One after another, they were carrying my hopes away into the uncaring night.

I began running with the train's flow, watching over my shoulder and praying for a break. Suddenly a dark slit surged toward me. I whirled and lunged. My forearms hooked a splintery floor, and the train's momentum yanked me from the ground. I threw out a frantic hand and dug for a grip as my legs flew back and under.

I couldn't hold on!

One foot bounced off the rail. The other one dragged gravel. Out of control, I yelled and clawed at the floor. Then my boot caught a cross tie and the whole world slid away. Suddenly the sky was the underside of a boxcar. Roaring wheels were in my face. Sparks were flying.

For a moment I lay stunned, tasting the wind of those terrible wheels. Then I rolled away with a cry and the stars came out again.

My arms were scraped, and my pants leg was wet with blood. But I didn't have any quit in me. I was up in sec-onds, running with the train again. I pushed hard through a haze of smoke and cinders, but the sinewy planks of the swaying wall still pulled away. Then I found a narrow shaft coming up from behind and I went for it.

This time I seized the edge of the sliding door. Again the train pulled me from the gravel. But now I had a firm grip and enough spring to throw my legs up and gain the rim. Still I was in awful danger, dangling there unable to fit through. But I forced the door open with my leg and fell inside.

I stood up in the blowing smoke and cinders. The car was reeling, and I could feel the rumble of the wheels through my boots. Across from me, a narrow shaft of moonlight fell through a crack. Otherwise, everything was as black as that stormy hollow in East Texas.

I took a step or two forward to escape the wind. Couplings floating with slack banged tight, throwing me into the wall. Jostled and battered, all I could do was sit down again and think about Pa.

"If you're ridin' in here, bo, chink the door so the bulls can't lock us in."

I jumped like a just-coupled boxcar. "Who's there?"

"Chink the door," the husky voice said again. "The stick's there beside you."

I remembered everything Wally had told me. The rails were a way of life for a lot of people these days. Hard times had robbed them of jobs, homes, and hope. Most of them were good men like Pa. All they wanted was a decent chance again. But every walk of life had its criminals.

I found a small limb at my boot and stood. The ghosts of trees were racing by now. I slid the door to, wedged the limb, and sat again. Now the bulls, or railroad policemen, couldn't secure the door quite so easily.

"Where ya headed, bo?"

This time the words were drunken and nasal, not raspy. That meant there were two men, maybe more.

"Said, 'Where ya headed?' You can hear, can't ya?"

I felt the boxcar lean away from a curve. "Austin, mister." No matter how hard I stared, all I could see was a moonlit strip of floor. With the bending of the train, the thin band of light had crawled to my boot. "Where y'all goin'?"

A gravelly laugh sounded from the far corner. "Just about anywheres the cops and bulls ain't at."

I caught nearby movement and a whiff of whiskey. One of them was approaching.

"Say," he said drunkenly, "ya wouldn't have a match on ya, would ya? Been tryin' to smoke this butt for the last hundred miles."

I scrunched up and ran my hand in my pants pocket. I'd just burned Old Man Jackson's brush pile the day before. "Let me see."

When I pulled out a match, something tumbled out with it. Suddenly my roll of dollar bills lay in that strip of moonlight for all to see. With as little of a show as possible, I retrieved it and stuffed it in my pocket.

"Here you go," I said, stretching out my hand in the dark.

The smell of whiskey grew stronger. "Where's it at?" he asked impatiently. "Gimme 'at thing."

His hand brushed mine, then grabbed my wrist. For a split second I was scared. Then he found the match and turned me loose.

The match flared. Past the cupped hands that lifted the flame to a cigarette, I met two hard, bloodshot eyes. They were set in a gaunt face with dark stubble and a scar at the jaw. Over in the corner sat another unkempt man. Then the match went out and there was only a cigarette glowing in the dark.

"Why, he ain't nothin' but a kid, is he?" said the farther man. "What are you doin' away from your daddy, anyhow?"

They both laughed, and I didn't like it. I was getting uneasy, and his words cut too deeply. I scooted back until the quaking wall was against my shoulders.

"Why, I don't think he wants to 'ssociate with us," slurred the man with the cigarette.

Trouble was brewing, and I knew it.

"No, I'm just kind of . . . kind of tired." I forced a nervous little laugh. "Trains sure can wear you out."

Suddenly the red ember was coming closer. I tensed like a coiled spring. "What do you want?"

"Well, listen, boy, we—"

"My father's here," I blurted. "He . . . he's on the ladder outside. He's fixin' to climb in."

A throaty laugh came from across the car. "Funny how you'd shut the door on him that way, ain't it?"

I came to my feet, and the ember rose with me. "He-he's gonna be here in a minute." I turned my face to the wind. "M-maybe I better go see about him."

"You ain't goin' nowhere, boy," snapped the drunken man.

"My father—he's fixin' to come in!"

"Well, it ain't your daddy I wanna do business with. Me and my buddy here's sure hard up. Ain't had no decent meal in—what is it now, three days?"

"Yeah—or a week," crackled the far voice, only now it wasn't so far.

"We was a-wonderin', boy," continued the man with the cigarette, "if you might loan us a little money to get us through."

I caught his partner's low, hoarse laugh. But now it came from right beside the ember.

I cringed. Pa needed that money—and I wouldn't give it to anybody but him!

"S-sorry, I ... I need everything I got."

"Give us that money!" snarled the throaty voice.

Fingers suddenly dug into my arm, but I ducked and squirmed free. I couldn't believe this was happening. It was like a nightmare. But the glowing ember rushing at me through the dark was real enough.

I reeled back and slammed into the end of the boxcar.

"I got ya, boy!" a voice growled in my face.

I dodged the ember and the drunken man hit the wall hard. Suddenly he had a vicious grip on my wrist.

He laughed cruelly. "Told ya!"

"The governor! I gotta see the governor! Let go of me!"

I twisted free with the panic of a cornered animal. As I did, my hand caught him hard in the teeth and the ember went out. I knew by his sharp cry that I'd accidentally flicked hot ashes in his face. He fell away, moaning and crying out something about his eyes.

"Where'd he go?" shouted the throaty voice.

But I had bought all the time I needed. I bolted across the car for the one place I knew they wouldn't follow. I slid open the door, faced the night, and jumped into a storm of wind and cinders and choking smoke.

Chapter 15

A Strange Peace

The wheels roared louder, and the gravelly slope flew up and hit me hard. The stars went to spinning crazily and I just started tumbling. I plowed through rocks and prickly pear and a lot of other things hidden by the night. I didn't have time to be afraid or think about all the hurt until I came to a stop against an algerita bush.

I lay there, stunned and groaning. I felt as if I'd lost all my hide and broken every bone. Then I tossed and squirmed, catching the movement of the train above. The speed of the thundering boxcars made me wonder how I'd lived through it. But that wasn't all I was thinking as I watched those cars hurtle into the night. They were carrying away our last chance to whip these hard times.

It had taken a fall from a windmill to clear Pa's head. A tumble from a barreling freight had finally opened my eyes, too.

Once and for all, the drouth had beaten us, and it was almost more than I could bear.

The rumble of the train had died in the distance before I forced myself up. I was skinned and bloodied, all right. But maybe I wasn't hurt all that badly, because everything seemed to work as I limped off the railroad right-of-way. Soon my boots found the caliche of a moonlit lane bordering the track.

Suddenly the whole world just seemed so terribly dark and hopeless. I'd let Pa down again! I'd let him down, and now we'd lost everything!

A shooting star streaked the sky, and I stopped and lifted my gaze. As I stared, a strange peace came over me. It was like a heavy burden lifting from my shoulders. The Lord was out there in those stars, and He was right here in our lives, too. I could accept our loss, because He was in control. Once again I'd tried to take things in my hands. Now they were back in His, where they belonged.

So what if we lost our home? In one sense, it had never really been ours. We had been just caretakers of it. Anyway, wasn't home more than dirt and lumber? What about all the sharing between people who loved each other? Wasn't that really what a home was, no matter where it took place?

Pa! Ma! Susie! They were waiting for me right now!

With a new spring in my step, I set out down the road for the only home that really mattered.

———⸙⸙———

On a peaceful night a few weeks later, we gathered around the dog-eared Bible for the last time in that sagging old house that my grandfather had built. The next morning we would board a train for Aunt Mildred's in Dallas and never come back to these dusty acres.

For the longest, we just sat clasping hands in that prayer circle—Pa, Ma, Susie, and I. I'll never forget the warmth of Pa's calloused palm as he finally spoke a simple prayer.

"Good Lord," he said, "we've had us some happy times here, but now You've seen fit to take us somewheres else. I ain't saying we're not wonderin' why. But we know You got Your got reasons and that they're good ones.

"We ain't got much left no more, Lord. We ain't got our cows, or a lot of our friends, or this old house. But we've got somethin' that makes all them other things not even matter no more. We got each other, Lord, and we got love. And there ain't *nothin'* can take that away."

He closed the prayer in our Savior's name. I looked up and found Ma and Susie smiling at me. But as I felt Pa's grip on my hand tighten and I turned to his eyes, I found his face the warmest of all.

We had lost a lot in those dark days of '34, all right. But maybe we had found even more.

———∿∿∾᷈᷈⊙᷈᷈᷈∾∿———

Six months later, Pa and Al Burke were working side by side in a Dallas factory and we had a place of our own to live. Ma was teaching a women's Bible study and Susie was playing with a new store-bought doll.

As for me, I was going to school and sitting beside my best friend—Shan! We had both matured a lot since Flat Creek. We weren't boyfriend and girlfriend anymore, but maybe that was better. This way, we could pal around and not worry about that romance stuff for a while. Besides, I liked being able to say hello without getting my tongue in knots.

I reckon we all had found plenty of reasons to be thankful.

The History Behind the Story

Hard times.

For many Texans in the 1930s, the Great Depression was more than just the greatest economic slump in United States history. It was a period of so little hope.

"It was *terrible* back in those depression days, I'll tell you," recalled the author's father, Delbert Dearen, in 1998. He was seventeen and living in Sterling City, Texas, when hard times struck in 1929. "There was no money and there were no jobs and there wasn't a whole lot of food. A lot of people went hungry and starved to death. Things were terrible, terrible, for twelve long years."

The decade after World War I gave little hint that disaster was on the way. The stock market rose sharply through much of the 1920s, and hopes were riding high. But all that changed on "Black Thursday" and "Black Tuesday" in late October 1929. The stock market crashed, ushering in an era of unprecedented hardship. Banks struggled. Factories folded. Businesses closed their doors.

As the depression wore on, company stocks on the New York Stock Exchange lost 89 percent of their value. Manufacturing dropped by 46 percent. Farm income fell by 50 percent. Wages fell by an average of 60 percent. Nine thousand banks failed, wiping out nine million savings accounts. As many as fifteen million people—three of every ten workers—found themselves without jobs. Bread and soup lines became common.

It is little wonder that people's hopes were clouded.

Although President Franklin D. Roosevelt tried to reassure Americans in 1933 that "the only thing we have to fear is fear itself," four million worried people took to the road or rails. Delbert Dearen, who once worked for only 50 cents a day and board in the early 1930s, was one of those.

He hopped his first freight train in Lamesa, Texas, in October 1933 and made a 360-mile journey that took him north to Lubbock, southeast to Sweetwater, and east on the Texas and Pacific Railroad to Fort Worth and Dallas. The Fort Worth train carried the hopes of a lot of struggling men, he recalled in 1982 and 1992.

> There were so many hoboes or bums on that train, I don't see how it untracked. They [the train men] couldn't have begun to think about throwing them off. There were all kinds of people, just out looking for work or trying to get home or somewhere else. Half of them probably didn't know where they were going or where they wanted to go. They were just trying to find some way to get by.

Many Texas families tried to tough it out on their farms, only to face barren skies and dusty fields. A lingering drouth in the 1930s was the worst in U.S. history. It spread like a blight across 75 percent of the nation and crippled portions of twenty-seven states.

Texas was among the hardest hit. In 1934 Comanche County, the setting for much of this novel, suffered through its second-driest year of the twentieth century. Peanut farmers stood by helplessly and watched their fields blow away. The Panhandle came under even greater trials, as twenty-two dust storms swept across 100 million acres of Texas, Oklahoma, New Mexico, Kansas, and Colorado. As these storms raged with increasing frequency, people began referring to this devastated region as the Dust Bowl. By 1937, another 180 "black blizzards" had choked the life from Panhandle croplands and driven 34 percent of its farmers from their homes.

"In the evenings the dust would come in, and you flat couldn't see nothing," recalled Ted Laughlin, who cowboyed north of Clovis, New Mexico, during the Dust Bowl days. "A particular man and I was riding along pretty close to a fence and a cloud come up, and a dust storm, too. Them horses couldn't even see one another; they'd just nicker. It was just as dark as it ever gets anywhere—no way you could see your hand in front of you."

Seven times between January and March in 1935, "dusters" reduced the visibility at Amarillo, Texas, to zero. One blackout lasted eleven and a half hours, and another storm savaged the region for three and a half days. The most infamous dust storm struck the Panhandle on "Black Sunday," April 14, 1935, when a boiling mass eight thousand feet high struck with a fury. At least 800,000 men, women, and children eventually fled the Dust Bowl, most of them bound for California.

Although President Roosevelt, in his first term, set in

motion many programs to combat the nation's woes, a real cure was still years away. "I see one-third of the nation ill-housed, ill-clad, ill-nourished," he said in his second inaugural address in 1937.

Dust Bowl families, in particular, continued to struggle, even as federal programs provided assistance. The Soil Conservation Service, created in 1935, taught farmers how to reduce erosion and planted almost 19,000 miles of trees to slow the wind. Still, sixty-one regional dust storms darkened the Dust Bowl in 1938.

With 15 percent of workers still unemployed in 1939, the nation gained a reprieve. Not only did autumn rains end the long drouth, but war erupted in Europe. American factories were deluged with orders from U.S. allies.

Conditions across Texas improved little by little over the next two years. Only thirty-four dust storms blanketed the Dust Bowl in 1940 and 1941, and with U.S. entry into World War II late in 1941, the nation mobilized. With massive demand for goods to support the war effort, the Great Depression finally ended.

For more information on the dark days from 1929 to 1941, check your library for these books: *Kids During the Great Depression,* by Lisa A. Wroble, and *Children of the Dust Bowl: The True Story of the School at Weedpatch Camp,* by Jerry Stanley. Also see the video *Riding the Rails.* For online photographs from the Great Depression and Dust Bowl era, check out the Library of Congress's American Memory website at *memory.loc.gov.*